Text Classics

ARTHUR GROOM was born in Caulfield, Melbourne, in 1904. His father, Arthur Champion Groom, was the member for Flinders in Australia's first federal parliament. The family moved to Queensland in 1911.

Groom worked as a jackeroo at Lake Nash station, near the Northern Territory border, before moving to Brisbane in 1926 to work for the *Sunday Mail*. His first book, *A Merry Christmas*, was published in London in 1930.

Groom was an avid walker and outdoor photographer. In May 1930 he founded the National Parks Association of Queensland and later became manager and jack-of-all-trades at Binna Burra guesthouse, on the edge of Lamington Park in south-east Queensland. During World War II Groom lectured Australian and American troops on jungle survival techniques.

He continued to write, but moved away from fiction: subsequent books focused on environmental protection, the conservation of Australia's great natural wilderness and tourism.

Groom died in Melbourne in 1953, three years after the publication of *I Saw a Strange Land*.

ALSO BY ARTHUR GROOM

A Merry Christmas
One Mountain After Another
Wealth in the Wilderness

I Saw a Strange Land
Journeys in Central Australia
Arthur Groom

Text Publishing Melbourne Australia

textclassics.com.au
textpublishing.com.au

The Text Publishing Company
Swann House
22 William Street
Melbourne Victoria 3000
Australia

First published by Angus and Robertson 1950
This edition published by The Text Publishing Company 2015

Cover design by WH Chong
Page design by Text
Typeset by Midland Typesetters

Printed in Australia by Griffin Press, an Accredited ISO AS/NZS 14001:2004
Environmental Management System printer

Primary print ISBN: 9781922182791
Ebook ISBN: 9781925095715
Author: Groom, Arthur, 1904–1953.
Title: I saw a strange land / introduced by Robyn Davison.
Series: Text classics.
Subjects: Groom, Arthur, 1904–1953—Travel.
Aboriginal Australians.
Northern Territory—Description and travel.
Australia, Central—Description and travel.
Dewey Number: 919.42904

This book is printed on paper certified against the Forest Stewardship
Council® Standards. Griffin Press holds FSC chain-of-custody
certification SGS-COC-005088. FSC promotes environmentally
responsible, socially beneficial and economically viable management
of the world's forests.

CONTENTS

Where Jehovah Visits
by Robyn Davidson

BEFORE HORSES and the wheel our species walked: heads up to survey the horizon, down to follow tracks and gather food. The human body's proprioception, its internal rhythm, is still geared to walking pace. We soothe our babies with it; our deepest understanding of time is measured by it. When we walk, the unconscious (the machinery that takes up most of the brain's effort) is free to do its work beneath the surface. Forget Rodin's sculpture—our best thinking is done on our feet.

There seems always to have been this intuitive connection between walking and cogitating. For the religious, pilgrimage healed the soul. The Greeks philosophised while strolling about. Aborigines went on walkabout as part of ceremonial life.

Where you walk matters as well. City walking is fine if you want to be overwhelmed by stimulus. But country walking, specifically spectacular-landscape walking, allows you to have, as Virginia Woolf put it, space to spread the mind out in.

There is a tremendous freedom in setting off on foot, with minimal fuss and baggage. The constraints of your life fall away, revealing a less cluttered self 'as pure as a polished shell', said the Buddha.

I know this because I did it myself, back in 1977. And, although unaware of it at the time, I followed in the footsteps of Arthur Groom, a young man who explored the 'amazing series of parallel ranges that wall the heart of Australia' thirty years before I did. *I Saw a Strange Land*, first published in 1950, is Groom's journal account of this trip. And if it were nothing more than lyric descriptions of the terrain he traversed, it would still be fascinating. Sometimes he uses camels to cart his gear, as I did, but mostly he carries what he needs on his back. He thinks nothing of trudging forty miles a day, or night. (You do not know what forty miles is until you have walked it: through sandhills, up and down plunging broken escarpments, along desiccated riverbeds.)

His evocations of the stupendous landscape uncovered memories that I had thought permanently buried. Muscle memories of scrambling over rocks and spinifex, of freezing dawns and hot days, of the unique intensity of being alone in a terrain that is surely among the most affecting in the world. Because I walked the landscape, slept on it, breathed it, drank it, I feel that, in some peculiar way, that country knows me. I am always homesick for it.

Groom even describes an experience I wrote about in my own journey-book, *Tracks*. A mournful, unaccountable sound, as of something haunting the air, sometimes far off, sometimes close. Both of us discovered (with relief) that it was the pre-dawn breeze, beginning in the high-up gorges, or in the tops of trees, while everything below remained perfectly still.

The range country of the Centre lends itself to those kinds of feelings. We are awed by its age, power and beauty; astonished at the play of light and colour; inhabited by atavistic reverence.

If Jehovah is anywhere, then surely he visits the chasms, escarpments and rivers of those primordial hills.

But ways of seeing are mediated by culture. Aboriginal people who belong there have, I imagine, a different aesthetic response. To them, all land is sacred, therefore it is all beautiful. Yet it was Albert Namatjira who first translated the Centralian colours to a European eye. Arthur Groom's meeting with the Great Man himself, and his talks with Namatjira's teacher, Rex Battarbee, form one of the many beguiling interludes in the book:

> Battarbee had been right. Here was natural colour beyond description. It was high up in the sky, with shades of blue and mauve reflected from the cliffs. It was in the patches of green spinifex, clinging in pinheads on the rubble slopes. It was in the water, the sand, even in the trees; and perhaps the slow-moving deep shadows were more colourful and mysterious than anything else. The colour was in the water-worn rocks of the river bed. There were boulders and slabs of green, grey, mauve, pink, white, red, black, and all the shades between. This colour system was entirely different to the bright colours of the canyon walls. It was of shades and tints, and went up about ten feet to normal flood level, proving that the basic colour of red was gradually being washed out of all the rocks crashing from above.

Groom worries about the effect tourism will eventually have on the area. Will graffiti be carved into the sandstone, or Aboriginal rock art be defaced? But, while it is likely that Jehovah makes himself scarce when buses full of tourists arrive at the better-known gorges and chasms of the MacDonnell Ranges, tourism, it turns out, has been the least of the desert's problems.

When I set off on my journey, many people thought I was mad; after it was over, I was constantly asked *why*. Even in 1946, Arthur Groom was thought a little odd, a man who walked when he did not have to.

The spark for his journey occurred, he tells us, twenty years before, when he was working as a jackaroo on a cattle station near the Queensland–Northern Territory border. He would have been about seventeen. Out of the eastern horizon a mirage appears: a tiny family and their sheep, heading into the 'elusive west', a visual archetype of striving pioneers. He neglects to ask the names of that 'insane family', but vows to one day find out their fate, and to do something 'as brave and big'.

His curiosity is also aroused by 'one hundred and fifty natives…dirty and diseased, hungry and miserable, the obvious remnants of a dying race' arriving from the opposite direction, out of the mythological west. He wonders 'what was being done to ease the passing of Australia's primitive man'. And so, a year after the end of World War II, he heads for Central Australia.

I find it impossible not to like Groom. You get the sense that he is a decent, somewhat naive young man, at the liberal end of the era's thinking. He is an early template for the conservationist, and something of a jack-of-all-trades. He is also a natural writer. His descriptions of landscape are in the Romantic mode, and his ear for dialogue is acute and charming. (The book is full of Aussie yarns—dry, comical anecdotes from the characters he comes across.) The scraps of history he weaves into his travels, and the light he casts on the assumptions and attitudes of the time, elevate his book above mere travelogue.

The first story he recounts is the epic of the Lutheran missionaries who journeyed into the desert to build a safe haven for Aborigines, and to teach them something of the Christian

God. It is a tale of staggering hardship and grit. Against all odds, they founded Hermannsburg Mission, which is Groom's first port of call out of Alice Springs. Here he discovers that the 'Aboriginal race' is not dying out after all.

In the 1920s Aborigines were still in the process of 'coming in' to missions and settlements from distant desert areas. Imagine it: the estates you have successfully managed for at least forty thousand years have been cut to pieces by hard-hoofed animals, invaded by new species of plant and predator, and colonised by people with technology derived from the transition to agriculture. The waterholes and soaks your survival depends on have been fouled by cattle, or used up by the camel trains delivering goods to 'the Outback'. Foxes, cats and rabbits are already doing tremendous damage to the productivity of your grounds. Bush tucker and indigenous animals are becoming scarce. Then comes a drought. The hunting-gathering economy unravels. And there are whitefella diseases, reprisals for killing stock or settlers, the odd massacre and, above all, hunger. In this unfolding catastrophe, missions and work-for-rations cattle stations provide basic security.

Groom does not quite seem to grasp how extraordinary it was that, while many of the 'pioneers' could not survive in the desert, Aborigines had managed to thrive. They were able to navigate vast areas of the desert using their understanding of nature, a knowledge welded into an entire poetic conception of reality. They were less technologically advanced, yet infinitely more developed at living in and using the natural world.

While he gives us a sense of the heroism of the missionaries, he cannot quite see that the Aborigines under their care are heroic on a grander scale. His interest in and sympathy for their plight is undoubtedly genuine but his tone can be excruciatingly paternalistic to a modern ear. Sometimes it's as if his perceptions struggle against the truisms he has absorbed. The truisms tend to win, but then, who can think and live too far outside the received thinking of their time?

We have the benefit of an intervening half century of scholarly research, and can hear the voices of Indigenous people themselves. Carl Strehlow recorded what he knew of their knowledge systems in 1915, but it wasn't until the 1950s and '60s that a plethora of publications on Aboriginal history and philosophy became widely available.

These days we can read our way into an appreciation of the intellectual feat of the Dreaming. It is not easy to understand. Sometimes I think that, if non-Indigenous Australians could truly comprehend the reach, complexity and sophistication of Aboriginal cosmology, we would fall on our knees in reverence to human ingenuity and imagination—the instinct towards meaning that unites us all.

I Saw a Strange Land reminds us how little life in the desert has changed. While cities on the seaboard hurtle into the future, constantly transforming themselves, Australia's remote areas seem hardly to alter at all. The screeching hordes of Aboriginal kids coming out to greet you, their high spirits at odds with the desolation of the camps; the failed, broken-down homesteads; the bogged cars and creaky old windmills—they are all still there. Any changes are subtle, and only observable to an experienced eye. Groom's account reveals how advanced the process of environmental deterioration was, even back then.

These days we rely almost totally on technology to find our way. When it fails us we become lost, literally and figuratively.

It's one thing to get lost in a town where help is nearby; it's quite another to do so when there is no way to reorient yourself. This happened to me once during my walk across the continent, and I will not easily forget the sudden enormity and indifference of the desert around me. The Australian desert is not a landscape to be taken lightly.

Nevertheless, my advice is to take *I Saw a Strange Land* for a very long walk. Use it as inspiration and guide. Go to the Larapinta Trail, let's say, a physically demanding but relatively safe introduction to the MacDonnell Ranges. Get out of the car. Ditch the GPS. Use your legs. Rediscover the primal link between walking and thinking. (But don't forget to take water.)

The Kangaroo Tail rock-slab, independent of the main bulk of
Ayers Rock, with figure for comparison. There is a space of
several feet between the slab and the mass.

ACKNOWLEDGEMENTS

Grateful acknowledgements are due to the officers of the Oxley and Mitchell Libraries, Brisbane; to the courtesy and assistance rendered by the Administrator of the Northern Territory, Mr A. R. Driver, and officers of the Administration; and to members of the Kodak staffs in Adelaide and Brisbane, who went to great trouble to provide and process photographic equipment. My thanks are due also to many Central Australian people whose hospitality will never be forgotten, particularly the missionaries at Hermannsburg; and to Tiger, a native, who showed outstanding attention to duty.

Some of the material has been published previously in article form by the *Courier-Mail*, Brisbane, the *Sun*, Sydney, the *Herald*, Melbourne, the *Advertiser*, Adelaide, the *Mercury*, Hobart, and the Australian Geographical Magazine, *Walkabout*. The encouragement rendered by these publications has been of considerable assistance.

Arthur Groom

This book is dedicated to a great task which commenced at Bethany, at 4pm, on 22 October 1875.

I Saw a Strange Land

CHAPTER I
CENTRAL AUSTRALIA TODAY

Mechanical transport has brought security and comfort to many in Central Australia, yet its roads have passed by some of the pioneers who battled vainly for a lifetime against drought and distance and loneliness. Their deserted homes and camps and broken stockyards bear mute testimony.

Camels, donkeys, and packhorses are now rare. Cars and trucks grind over hundreds of miles of rocky desert, sandy desert, or fertile plain; and the average man's vehicle is a heavy truck ready equipped with drums of water and petrol, and food and swag for any long, sudden journey. Many of the old camel and packhorse mail services are now replaced by Eddie Connellan's little planes, centred at Alice Springs, jumping like grasshoppers in a fortnightly service over distances from a few miles up to hundreds of miles, from station to station, Mission depot, or mining-field; and many of the native watchers whose keen eyes once saw the ground mail approaching slowly, hours before its arrival, now attune their ears to the sky, and yell at the faintest distant drone of a powerful engine, 'Hareyplane come up sit down now. Gottem mail-bag for ebbrybody!'

The transceiver – the two-way radio and telephone transmitter and receiver – has become the speedy messenger of good and bad tidings; and far-out homes may talk several times a day with Alice Springs, and Alice Springs talks and listens to the rest of the world. Pioneers still toil and sweat away in the wild places beyond all roads. They always will be out beyond journey's end as long as ambition and hope rule in the hearts of men; but many of the Old Hands have turned out their camels and packhorses, and have become mechanized.

Most of the natives have moved in from far-out hunting grounds, and now dream of the past in the shelter of ration depots, Mission stations, cattle and sheep homesteads and camps; and many of them have grown fond of the white man's sweet and artificial foods.

The town of Alice Springs, well planned, and set almost in the heart of Australia, has grown rapidly from the wild and isolated, yet friendly Overland Telegraph Station of years ago, into a modern centre of two thousand people. It dominates half the Northern Territory of Australia, and its influence spreads across the continent. It is 'the Alice' to all within hundreds of miles. It has an ultra-modern post-office, a large rambling hospital with insufficient staff, an important radio and Flying Doctor base. There are bitumen roads through most of the planned town area, concrete paths and drains, electric light and power, a modern concrete jail near the hospital; many bulk warehouses and modern shops, cafes, beauty parlours and billiard saloons, and the inevitable second-hand joints. There are two open-air picture shows, freezing cold in winter and melting hot in summer. The town has only two hotels, and a third being built up in concrete above all the other buildings in town. There are monuments, but no public hall, and the best place to greet a dignitary is where you first say good day to him. There are workshops, trucking yards, orchards, schools, abattoirs, and poultry farms, a sandy golf-course, race-course, tennis courts floodlit at night, sports-grounds, cricket and football fields out on the open clay-pans; and an all-night café serving omelettes and meals in the wee small hours to those who have to be entertained, or filled for the long road ahead or behind. The streets are lined by day with heavy motor-trucks and trailers, light trucks, utilities, and comparatively few touring cars fussing about like rare polished toys against the giant transports. Everyone seems to have 'come in' from somewhere, hundreds of miles perhaps, or is ready to 'go out' a hundred or a thousand miles. The sandwich bar in the main street sells sandwiches by the hundred 'for the road', and over at 'The Chows'', tea and sandwiches or a three-course meal may be had in a dim interior with all its memories of the past.

Alice Springs has a steam laundry and collection and delivery service. It runs its own newspaper, the *Centralian Advocate*. It has a town water-supply and storage pumped up into large steel tanks on the hundred-foot height of Billy Goat Hill beside the railway yards, separated from Nanny

5

Goat Hill by the odd Todd River of sand and leaning river gums a hundred yards wide, and never the twain shall meet!

Drought may overlook a year or two in time and weather, and blast destruction and hot sand over the land; but in its departure it will set a flood trap to confound the unwary who doubt it will rain again. It is then that the Todd floods, and Alice Springs people protest and cry loudly to the Administration for bridges and water conservation, as millions of gallons swirl through Australia's strangest river gateway two miles southward of the town, and on and on, to disappear in desert sand away to the south-east.

It would seem that many millions of years ago a mammoth force cut straight down with a cleaver and slit the main ridge of the Macdonnell Ranges to its base, and ordained that some day all travelling things, whether mechanical, animal, human, or bird, and even the waters themselves, should crowd between the red cliffs less than a hundred yards apart. Bitumen highway, railway line, power and phone lines, were built by men beside the sandy river whose bed is the stock route; and the airliners, going over daily, sight the gap from afar and fly above it. But east and west of Heavitree Gap there are larger and deeper gaps in the amazing series of parallel ranges that wall the heart of Australia. The barrier effect dividing north and south is so definite and impressive that one might expect to find a lost nation over the other side.

Within Heavitree Gap all sounds are magnified, and echoes of train or truck or plane above, rumble deeply. Millions of years ago, Central Australia was elevated in great plateaux, sloping and draining gently southward, until tremendous expansion from afar, and horizontal pressure over a great distance, pushed the landscape upward in gigantic corrugations.

In the Old Days the scientist was the main visitor of the month or year. The scientists who come and go now, do so quietly; overshadowed by Alice Springs' annual crop of winter tourists, arriving by plane daily, or by train each Saturday up from Adelaide to friendly greeting and flurry of local curiosity; or sometimes by car or truck up via the long, lonely, rough and difficult desert road from the south, or down by the Great Northern bitumen highway from Darwin. They seek exciting adventure described in tourist folders, and find that a modern town has risen above the graves of the earliest settlers. They wander in bewilderment, looking, perhaps, for the things written of years ago. They learn to like Alice Springs' dry, clear, winter climate, and the neat homes and lawns, flowers, and orange-trees, the drooping pepperinas; and the modern school with its pupils in all the known shades from black to white. They like the clean bitumen streets, and the big gum-trees left in the centre of the main thoroughfares. They stand and look at the modern hostels for aborigines and for white people, and admire the thrilling insignia above the Flying Doctor's white stone gateway, glaring in contrast against the pink and red of Mount Gillen, a mile or so southward. There is the contrast of the modern business-man just up by plane to talk insurance with the Old Pioneer and all his friends and family. Over all, there is a friendliness that has never died out from the Old Days, but has sorted itself into cliques and groups in business and private life;

and a new, and sometimes humorous or frantic interest in public welfare.

Some day, Central Australia's transition period will form a pattern. It was emerging from the old order and gathering *tempo* when Japan's treachery in the Pacific gave it military importance, and rapidly modernized the locality of the town in contrast to the surrounding wilderness of desert and plain, and high rugged mountains with hidden waters. General Douglas MacArthur flew non-stop from the Philippines and landed at Alice Springs; and thousands of people who have forgotten the name of the town still remember the event.

The future of Alice Springs has gripped its people. Everyone is now civic planner and critic in one, and the town buzzes with nebulous schemes. It is proof of civic pride, and many of the old-timers wonder where it will all lead to, for already the pubs are often overcrowded with tourists, and some old-timers find that the beds, once saved automatically for rare visitors into town from far out, are now occupied by pale-faced people in city clothes and collar and tie.

The sandy banks of the Todd are still good to camp on.

You drive now from the bitumen roads of the town area, straight out onto desert sand or rocky wilderness in one or another direction, as suddenly as going through a gate. The exception is the bitumen Sturt Highway, built as a wartime necessity from the large aerodrome six miles south of Alice Springs, nearly one thousand miles north-ward to Darwin.

Sand and erosion have obliterated many of the old

camel pads that lead through deep mountain passes, and mechanical transport has chosen new routes. Much of Central Australia's scenery is now panoramic, from a window; and often viewed from a distance in a passing show of blue and purple shadows, dominated by masses of towering red rock.

ABOVE: A quarter of a mile wide, the mighty Finke sweeps into the Krichauff Range. The white strip to the right of the river is the motor track to Palm Valley.

BELOW: Sandhills within fifty yards of Henbury Station homestead.

ABOVE: Hermannsburg Mission, beside the Finke River, showing the large vegetable-garden compound tended by native women.

BELOW: Native rock-hole in a once 'ceremonial' valley near Hermannsburg Mission.

CHAPTER II
TWENTY-FIVE YEARS AGO

From January 1922 until June 1925 I worked at Lake Nash Cattle Station on the eastern side of the Northern Territory, adjoining the Queensland border. Geographically, the several thousand square miles of Lake Nash country were cut off from the rest of the Northern Territory by eighty miles of spinifex desert to westward, and small strips of mallee and clay-pan desert to north and south.

From the lovely Aghadaghada Waterhole at the western end of Lake Nash run, an old camel pad led out over the 'eighty miles dry'; and stories were legion of the many tons of mica that had been camel-packed in from Hatch's Creek west of the desert. There was the story of the full-sized piano that had 'gone out' from Queensland on the back of an old bull camel, only to be eaten by white ants and filled with shifting sand. Round the campfires in the stock camps

I listened, and heard tales of Blue Bob the B—, of Dancing Paddy the Irishman, of the Harbour Master, who named all the ducks on a waterhole after tugs in the Brisbane River, and of Sandover Bill, who was credited with driving thirty-six bullocks to Adelaide, himself mounted on a lonely cow camel; of Jumping Jack the Poisoner, the Tropical Frog and the Old Waterhen, Tin-toe Harry, the Kynuna Lady, and Billy the Pig; and scores of others whose idiosyncrasies named them.

But they were all men of the elusive West, which is always west of where the tales are told, at least one more day's travel beyond tomorrow.

We had mustered and were holding nearly two thousand mixed cattle near Elditta Waterhole on Gordon's Creek. It was midday, and warm for June, with dancing mirages that rolled blackly across the plain to northward and burst in dazzling waves against dark gidyea forests. Some miles to eastward we noticed a grotesque sprawling movement. It was too slow to be a car caught in the mirage; and it was much too large and wide. It twisted and cavorted over some hundreds of yards of ground. Not a mob of cattle, surely? No one else had any right to muster on the Lake Nash run. Not horses? Where would they be going? It all rose and fell and squirmed as one broad mass, confounding our early guesses, until a covered vehicle drawn by two horses, emerged from the distortion, became definite and moved up beside a flock of several hundred sheep and goats.

A hundred questions presented themselves to us, and we left the cattle with native boys and rode across to intercept the strange convoy. Where were they going? This was

11

Albert Namatjira, the famous full-blooded aboriginal watercolour artist.

North-east from the crest of the Ellery Ridge in the Macdonnells.
The black dots are mostly mulga-trees in gullies between spinifex ridges.

not a normal stock route. Someone lost, off his course, many miles west of any known sheep country. No sheep had ever passed that way before. The sight was almost unbelievable. Two children were riding ponies and droving the mixed herd. A woman drove the old vehicle. She had two small children beside her. Several bantams squawked in a coop slung beneath the van. We questioned the man who appeared to be in charge. What was he doing? Where was he going? Didn't he know there was desert beyond the Aghadaghada Waterhole, and only camels had gone out before in the direction he was heading?

His answers were simple and astounding. Yes, he knew of the desert. He had been nearly six months on the road from Mungindi on the border of Queensland and New South Wales; and he was going 'out' to the Sandover River country, east of the Overland Telegraph Line. He had chosen a locality on a map that showed only broad white space, crossed by the uncertain, unknown, broken lines of the Sandover River, so little known that is was still a mystery whether its rare waters went south-west or north-east!

He intended to take up land somewhere 'out there', and breed sheep in defiance of all the accepted beliefs and principles. He had faith in himself and his family. They were all in it together, and all knew that a tough time lay ahead.

And that was all there was to it. Surely it was utter lunacy, yet his remarks were simple and convincing, almost terrifying, and left us entirely without answer. We persuaded him to accept fresh beef; and the strange procession moved slowly on across the flat red clay-pans beside Gordon's Creek, and on in the direction of the last known water at Aghadaghada, sixty miles away.

It was not until a mirage to the westward had spread once more like a dancing octopus, and engulfed them all, that we realized we did not know the man's name.

That night, and many other nights, I sat beside a campfire, and thought of that brave insane family. It brought a craving to do something just as brave and big. Dead west there was little known settlement before Barrow Creek Telegraph Station on the Overland Telegraph Line, two hundred and fifty-five miles by air. In between, the Sandover River wandered vaguely through desert land; its course was known to move north and south to the vagaries of uneven seasons. We had mustered cattle well out beyond the Aghadaghada Waterhole, and had always turned back at the beginning of a land known to very few, but often spoken of by natives as 'Eighty miles dry country – no water.'

Weeks and months went by, and no word came through. A few wandering natives reported tracks west of Aghadaghada, and well out over the desert; but rain had fallen and covered all tracks beyond. It was the only good news in a story of faith and grit that might have finished without an ending.

It happened in June 1923.

Months later, in the full heat of summer, the desert west of Lake Nash Station was crossed again; but this time up from the south-west and over a long curve towards the east. My wood-cutting camp was beside a small muddy pool, seventy miles west of the homestead. I rose one hot morning to find that nearly one hundred and fifty natives

13

had 'come in' during the night, stealthily and unseen, and were camped about in small groups. They were dirty and diseased, hungry and miserable, the obvious remnants of a dying race. There was little I could do for them. I could obtain no coherent story; but they spoke of Lunderundtera and Ilgulla Waterholes, and of Arltunga, one hundred and fifty miles to the south-west. It appeared that they were not wanted somewhere, and had been warned off. They had come through to an area new and strange to them, tired, dispirited, and lethargic. They knew nothing of the white man and his family who had gone west six months before, and my attempts to describe a flock of sheep to them were hopeless.

A few weeks later heavy rain set in, filled up gaping thirsty cracks, and bogged the plains. The small water-course known as Vivey's Creek ran a banker, and then suddenly swelled and rumbled with a far greater volume of water than the restricted watershed of Vivey's would allow. I knew then that somehow the Sandover had flooded, and found an old or a new course to the east.

Once again I began to wonder what had happened to the man and his family who had gone west half a year before. It was one of those persistent, unanswered questions of youth that often decide the pathway of the man.

In 1925 I left the eastern side of the Northern Territory and wandered down to Brisbane. Two unanswered questions went with me, and persisted throughout the years. Some day I would go back, and possibly a long way farther back behind the desert west and south of Aghadaghada; and possibly I would find out the name of the man who had taken faith and loyalty and crossed the desert; and even more important, perhaps, I might find out what was being done to ease the passing of Australia's primitive man.

CHAPTER III
MUSICAL INTERLUDE

The opportunity to return to Central Australia did not occur until the winter of 1946. By then many more questions had cropped up, and I felt that some of the answers might be found at Alice Springs. I had read accounts and studied rough maps of its surrounding mountains rising to nearly five thousand feet. Mountains of such height must be separated by ravines and wild watercourses; and there would be hidden valleys between towering cliffs, and many mysterious places beyond the ordinary travel of man.

And thus I wanted to see if Central Australia's scenery was grand enough, the climatic conditions moderate enough, to warrant tourist development in any large degree; and I wanted to find out what degree of protection over the native men and women and the wilderness areas they roamed in, might be necessary to preserve intact the heart of our continent for the education and benefit of future generations.

On Australia's Victory Day of June 1946 I flew by airliner from Brisbane one thousand two hundred and ninety-eight miles to Adelaide; and then, after a few hours' rest in noisy Adelaide while its people still frolicked in the streets, I went up again before dawn into the dark void above the city's lights. The plane circled widely and thrummed up into heavy cloud. It muffled the engines. We had a full list of passengers and crew. The man beside me had scored a window seat; he stretched about six and a half feet of body and limbs and settled down to ignore the daylight when it came; and mumbled quite a lot about needing at least a week of sleep to recover from the Victory celebrations.

Daylight crept in and grew strong. Then we broke the clouds and flew up into the sun. I reached awkwardly across the sleeper and wiped the window, which had become moist with vapour, and looked down on Australia's inland pattern, now clearly coloured desert.

Red, pink, brown, and grey rock, sand, and earth struggled to conquer diminishing belts of forest. As we sped northward into brightness of colour and deeper blue sky, the red gradually dominated all colours and became the base upon which all the land patterned itself. White-rimmed salt lakes, some of them azure blue and sometimes grey or green towards the centre, sometimes clear with large patches of gleaming white sand, stood out against the dominant red. We went down on to the Mount Eba aerodrome in its tremendous isolation west of the long railway stretching up from Adelaide to Alice Springs. It is a pebbly landing field, with a radio station, a large nearby wool-shed, and a near and far panorama of billions of small oval red pebbles, over which I walked for warmth in the cold, bright winter sunlight. A little old man with a peaked beard manipulated a noisy putt-putt engine and refuelled our plane; then a cheery call from the pilot, and up into the high glare of sun again through a bumpy roughness at about one thousand feet, then into the calm of almost imperceptible movement at ten thousand feet, heading north.

Australia's heart opened wider. Away to the northeast, water flashed and died slowly out where recent rain had filled a large clay-pan lying between giant sandhills that continued over the horizon.

We circled Oodnadatta and landed; then up and on again, this time high above Simpson's Desert, tremendous, and patterned in more detail than the most delicate embroidery. There were eroded gullies and narrow ravines, odd pinnacles and small plateaux and, as we went farther north, a curious repetition of parallel ridges, low at first, but gradually more definite and prominent. Delicate detail and hazy detail merged into distance towards every horizon. It was a glorious land of colour from the air, but a land of thirst and terrible hardship for those who might try to cross its surface.

Dry watercourses, like paralysed green serpents, twisted in from the west, crossed beneath, and continued south-east towards the Lake Eyre cesspit of spent rivers.

The southern approach to Alice Springs, nine hundred and eighty-one miles north of Adelaide, is dramatic. A high red wall of rock, topped with green spinifex, bars the way. We landed at the aerodrome just before noon, four miles south of this Macdonnell Ranges wall. I had travelled 2,279 miles in thirty-six hours, which included fifteen hours' flying time at an average of 152 miles per hour. My sleepy companion decided to come with me to put in a four-day 'snooze' at the Stuart Arms Hotel before continuing by air to Darwin. He had slept in the plane and now he dozed in the motor-coach and did not hear the echoing rumble as we whizzed through Heavitree Gap. We shared a room at the rambling old hotel. He remained upright for lunch, and then coiled up in a bed much too short for his long legs.

Pastor Philip A. Sherer, of the United Evangelical Lutheran Mission at Hermannsburg, knocked on my door, introduced himself, and tactfully asked the purpose of my visit and offered all the assistance in his power. I explained my interest in the protection of primitive wilderness areas, particularly in its relation to the future of nomadic natives. He begged me not to walk straight off alone through the Macdonnell Ranges, as I had planned, but to go with him to Hermannsburg Mission and get helpful advice from the Superintendent, the Reverend F. W. Albrecht. I liked Sherer. He was young and keen. The modern term is that we 'clicked', and jabbered away like a pair of parrots. He introduced me to the Reverend A. C. Wright, Superintendent of the Ernabella Presbyterian Mission at the eastern end of the isolated Musgrave Ranges. Mr Wright looked like an old prospector; we found him a mile out, dismantling an army hut for removal to Ernabella, three hundred miles by rough sandy road south-west of Alice Springs. He was cautious, and could not see readily any essential connecting link between protection of scenery and aboriginal welfare. I left him, feeling that he would chew the subject over and appreciate it.

During the war many defence buildings were erected in Alice Springs in a hurry. I entered one, now cleared of its wartime furniture. Tables and chairs had disappeared from the polished brown floor, and apparently the telephone mechanic was not far behind, for disused telephones stood up oddly all over the floor. I found Mr V. R. Carrington, Acting Administrator, and Mr Arthur R. Driver, the new Administrator, in a far corner. I asked for a permit to enter the Aboriginal Reserves.

Permits are hard to get, and probably one of many important reasons is that there are a few well-meaning people, mostly motherly women, who think that their presence in an Aboriginal Reserve with a large bag of lollies would solve all the problems of the native races.

I was granted a permit on condition that I entered the Aboriginal Reserves under the supervision of the missionaries at Hermannsburg. It at least gave me a wide range of possible movement.

My room-mate at the hotel slept on. Entry and exit to and from the room did not waken him. I groped about, wrapped and rewrapped parcels, and eventually concluded he was an easygoing chap who would work and sleep a lot up in Darwin, and keep well within the town's boundary.

Several Adelaide people were spending winter in Central Australia. They swapped yarns, opinions, and experiences round a small fireplace in the hotel's small music-room. They had many ideas for Alice Spring's future. One retired business-man was deeply interested in the town's permanent alcoholics, and worked on a theory that men drank only when there was nothing better to do. He had organized evening talent concerts, which were to a certain extent successful in bringing together singers, poets, clowns, a couple of magicians, and an excellent pianist whom I first noticed lying dead to the world on the concrete pavement outside the sandwich bar opposite the hotel.

The concerts were held in the music-room, which was about fourteen feet square and had only one narrow door and no window. For my last night in town the pianist put on a good turn on the badly tuned old piano; then two tenors excelled themselves, and there was a temporary lull that was shattered by a violent blare of ear-splitting noise when a man greeted as 'Mac' planted himself in the doorway and blew a cornet with all the force he could muster. He reddened and dribbled and swayed and tottered, but we could not stop him. His face bulged; he tossed the cornet up and down, round and round, doubled and twisted with all the artistic contortions of a man who knows no equal. The noise was deafening, and after some agonizing minutes of shattering torture some of his mates led him off to the hotel bar, from where the cornet sounded only in spasmodic outbursts. A bearded dwarf eventually returned and reported that Mac's legs had given way, and they had him 'down' in the bar, and drinks were being passed to him in quick succession as the only way of shutting him up. In the end there was a violent gurgle and outburst of language, and the latest news-flash wag returned to inform us that

21

someone had poured a pot of beer into the cornet, and that Mac was 'out' to it.

Silence settled over the hotel, and we trooped off over to the sandwich bar for supper of tea and toast. The place was crowded with tourists, townspeople, and hungry travellers whose trucks, cars, wagons, horses, camels, and stock were parked anywhere within a mile or two.

At about 3 a.m. the sound of Mac's cornet wakened half the town. He had tottered to the hotel woodheap, and beneath a large pepperina-tree, and by the light of a late moon, he played his agonizing notes to a fleet of heavy transport trucks loaded with surplus war material from Darwin.

With Pastor Sherer driving, and Rex Battarbee, the watercolour artist, and several of his native art pupils clinging to the top of a loaded three-ton truck, I left Alice Springs at noon. The truck was loaded with stores, and the usual 44-gallon water- and petrol-drums. Battarbee is tall and gaunt, with sharp features, somewhat shy and reserved, but always ready to give reliable information. He pointed out watercourses and wide valleys through the mountains; and named the summits, the trees and bushes, and each branching track or route of the past and present: turn-off to Simpson's Gap goes *that* way – Temple Bar Gap's down there to the south – the biggest ghost gum in the country is a mile or so up to the right, and was once painted in watercolour by Albert Namatjira, aboriginal full-blood – the sharp blue peaks ahead are north of Standly Chasm, and the domed height is Mount Conway, named by the explorer Ernest Giles in 1872, after Mr Conway of the early

Peake Cattle Station – Jay Creek runs down *this* side of Conway.

It was all very helpful. We stopped for a while at the Government Aboriginal Depot at Jay Creek, in the charge of Mr and Mrs Ringwood. The house is built of concrete, and stands in a garden of fruit-trees, vegetables, and flowers; and a mile beyond it, beside the dry, sandy creek, is the native settlement of ration store, huts, and little iron church, surrounded by untidy wurlies. We continued on, out through a low gap in the Macdonnell Ranges, and on to the broad Missionary Plain. Battarbee identified more peaks and ranges. There was now a sharp deep blue and mauve about Conway, with Paisley's and Brinkley's Bluffs beyond, to continue on, peak after peak and curve after curve – the amazing Macdonnells in full marching order from East to West. The Waterhouse Range lay down to the south, low and crouching on the plain, but shimmering brown and light red. It is a place of great interest to geologists, who know it as a great dome about six miles across, kidney-shaped when seen from the air, about forty miles long, and hollowed in the centre down to the level of the surrounding plain by the relentless erosion of millions of years. It contains an excellent example of a 'pound' – the term given to these larger hollowed centres surrounded by the remaining outer walls of a mountain that was once high and massive.

We crossed the sandy Hugh River, one-time route of the Overland Telegraph Line, which was completed in 1872. The river heads north of the Macdonnells, and cuts its way southward through range after range to meander across the

Missionary Plain, then winding sharp and deep through the centre of the Waterhouse. John McDouall Stuart found it, and trudged slowly and patiently along its sandy banks in April 1860, while on his first exploration over the heart of Australia; and his footsteps followed up and down beside it again and again, until he must have known every bend by heart. Thirty miles dead south of the Waterhouse the Hugh slashes through the brilliant-red ridges of the James Range, and then continues south-east in a twisting course for about another eighty miles before joining the grand old Finke.

At sunset, Rex Battarbee pointed out the gleaming rich red of Mount Hermannsburg, the deep purple shadows of the Finke River Canyon, and the red rock masses of the James and Krichauff Ranges behind. He advised me to memorize Mount Hermannsburg well, for it was an important landmark, and lay a couple of miles south-west of the Mission. Early arrival before darkness was delayed by a bad blow-out, and Pastor Sherer and I wrestled with nuts and jacks beneath the heavily laden truck; and it was by the light of a strong moon gleaming over the plains and the winding Finke River and slumbrous hills beyond, that we rolled down the sandy Aerodrome Hill, and slid between Mission buildings to the Superintendent's long stone bungalow, where a babbling crowd of native children and adults milled excitedly about the truck and clambered over everything. My hand was gripped again and again, sometimes enthusiastically, sometimes cautiously, timidly; and there seemed no end to it, and to the muttered and laughing 'Good days', until I was ushered into the house.

The Reverend F. W. Albrecht, Superintendent since 1929 of the Hermannsburg Mission of the United Evangelical Lutheran Church of Australia, reminded me of Charles Laughton the actor, thick-set and of medium height, he walked with a limp. Albrecht was born in Poland and trained as a missionary at the little church town of Hermannsburg in Germany. He was sent out to Australia with his wife for the sole purpose of making things a little easier for a race of primitive people condemned to segregation and slow extinction by the march of civilization. He landed as a man inexperienced in bush and desert ways, without mastery of the English language. Nearly a century before, many of his countrymen had migrated to South Australia, and had made good, and Mission work among the dispossessed natives had presented itself to them as a very practical form of thanksgiving for their new freedom.

Albrecht is respected throughout Central Australia, and by all anthropologists. He battled from the first as a complete stranger in a tough land, handicapped by drought and heat and bitter winter frost, and by rare floods that could destroy with water all that drought had spared. The Reverend Carl Strehlow before him, and earlier pioneer missionaries, had set a high standard of work against all the handicaps of a distant outpost; but Albrecht stuck tight to the job, learnt the languages of the Arunta* and Pitjentjara tribes, and the lore of the bush and wilderness and desert spaces, and grew to understand their moods. He has beaten through much red tape, and defied the cry

* Aranda.

25

from some quarters that it would be more humane to let a doomed race die out in any case; until now he stands as one of the main reasons why the primitive people west of the centre line of Australia may even yet survive and increase. He has tremendous capacity for hardship and work, and is gifted with sound breadth of vision and understanding of people and their problems.

In daylight, the Mission, its older buildings, and the natives are at first disappointing. The glamour and camouflage of a moonlight arrival the night before had vanished completely. The buildings showed the ravages of sand and drought and time. There was no planned entrance to the Mission: its front and back faced in all and every direction from a central street or compound; and the original clay-pans of the chosen site had been churned into loose sand by busy feet, as though thousands of cattle had stampeded. In all directions except an arc in the north, untidy native wurlies were scattered near at hand and as far as half a mile distant. They were roughly built of bits of material from scraps of iron to scraps of canvas, bagging, and bushes, the focal points of dogs and odd donkeys and camels.

But the worst of the picture passes as yelling, chattering life and laughter take over; the drabness and the trampled, untidy surroundings hide an amazing story of devotion and sacrifice, laughter amid tears, and infinite patience in Christian effort, which has seldom been equalled.

The native children are generally healthy with a harum-scarum scurry and freedom of their own design in play, and with a bare-faced curiosity towards visitors. They were up in trees, on the old roofs, lining up in long queues to be fed, sliding down slippery slides, swinging like monkeys from parallel bars; they were on merry-go-rounds, riding and falling off donkeys amid continuous laughter, rounding up camels and cattle and goats just to let them loose again. They were in and out of every workshop and outhouse, running helter-skelter after old tyres or an old ball, throwing small spears and boomerangs, and stalking imaginary game and going through all the movements and sounds of a 'kill'; all with a vitality possible only to youth in its element, until school-time, when there was a certain lessening of the babble and scramble; and old Community Leader Abel*, black as the ace of spades behind his sheer white moustache, made his round of law and order and checked the first relay of kids off towards the sandy parade-ground at the base of a tall pole flying the Union Jack. Here and there a bleary-eyed, dirty child stood quietly with matted hair and tattered clothes – a myall, just in perhaps for the first time from many miles out, puzzled and still a little frightened, in his first contact with an outpost of civilization. Tomorrow he might be gone again with his parents into the wilderness; or he might stay. The freedom of the nomad was his, and the call of his primitive forefathers still strong and definite; but the white man's foods were sweet and tempting.

I kept thinking back to the summer of 1923, and to the pitiful remnant band of unwanted natives who had crossed desert country to Lake Nash. The contrast presenting itself

---

* Pronounced 'Ah-bel'. A in Arunta, Aranda, or Arandta is usually spoken a 'Ah'.

27

at Hermannsburg was unexpected. This was no dying race – there were too many children. I asked the Reverend F. W. Albrecht to tell me the whole story, for I had believed the work of Missions to be nothing more than a merciful delaying of the final death of the aboriginal race.

CHAPTER IV
THE AUSTRALIAN
FREEDOM OF WORSHIP

In February 1835 the British Government set up a Board of South Australian Commissioners, including George Fife Angas, a London merchant and shipowner, and founder of the National Provincial Bank of England and the Union Bank of Australia.

Angas bought up large areas of South Australian land, and from 1838 onwards migrated chosen groups of Europeans. In 1838 he sent out five hundred Lutherans, victims of German persecution, who landed in South Australia and settled on new land north of Adelaide. Another group of Lutherans landed and settled at Nundah, in the Moreton Bay district of New South Wales, now within the State of Queensland.

The Lutherans were industrious, deeply religious;

and the hardships of a strange new land made success a common goal, if only to repay the faith of their sponsor, George Fife Angas, who had a deep sympathy with them in their search for freedom of worship. Angas did not come out to live in South Australia until 1851. By then he had assisted in migrating over eight thousand Lutherans. Eventually the Lutherans founded a Mission Board to foster work amongst dispossessed natives, as a thanksgiving for religious freedom in a new land. In 1866 a start was made at Kaporamanna on Cooper's Creek, between Birdsville and Marree. The Lutherans divided into two Synods. One controlled the Kaporamanna Mission; the other Synod began to look much farther afield. It was then that their spiritual leader, Pastor Heidenreich, called on Surveyor-General Goyder of Adelaide. Goyder pointed to a blank area in the heart of Australia, saying that he recommended it as a site for a far-out Mission among aborigines for these reasons: (a) the adjacent Macdonnell Ranges to northward, and the James and Krichauff Ranges twenty miles to southward, would form natural boundaries for limited numbers of Mission stock; (b) the few known waters of the Finke River facilitated the movements of large numbers of natives.

The information had been gathered from the notes of Ernest Giles, who had turned west from John McDouall Stuart's cross-continent exploration route of 1862. During the early summer months of 1872 Giles had traversed much of the inhospitable wilderness west and south-west of the Macdonnell Ranges. His diary recorded a land of parallel hills, mysterious creeks, and sandy rivers in which water might sometimes be found by digging.

ABOVE: In Palm Valley, Krichauff Range. The palm to the left
is one of the rare *Livistona Mariae*.

BELOW: Fallen red boulders of sandstone in Palm Valley.

ABOVE: Glen Helen homestead, beside the Finke River.

BELOW: The ridges of the Macdonnells on the southern side of the
Glen Helen Valley. The crest of this ridge is about eight hundred feet high.

In 1875 Pastor F. A. H. Kempe and Pastor W. F. Schwarz, newly ordained and young, arrived in South Australia and reported to Pastor Heidenreich; and after only six weeks there, set out with Shepherd Mirus, 33 horses, 17 cattle, and 3100 sheep from the little village of Bethany near Tanunda, at 4 p.m., after a prayer-meeting and blessing, in the crackling summer heat of 22 October. Only blind ignorance and tremendous faith could have overlooked the incredible mistake of sending such an inexperienced and cumbersome expedition northward into the continent's little-known dry interior. Men and animals were to battle for nearly two years through drought, heat, starvation, bitter winter cold and exposure, and the resultant sick-nesses of blight and scurvy; but ever northward, and ever so slowly, right up into the heart of the continent, over which the new and costly Overland Telegraph Line stretched like a shimmering black thread along its thousands of poles. They were not long behind the explorers Gosse (1873) and Giles (1872–5). Giles had been able to travel with some speed. His experienced party had been limited to Messrs Carmichael and Alexander Robinson, fifteen chosen horses, and a humorous pup. They had no cattle or sheep to impede them.

Schwarz and Kempe moved slowly through Siegersdorf, Kapunda, Allendale, and on to Waterloo, where they gladly purchased a harness horse for £40 to replace a cantankerous animal that had been kicking its wagon harness to bits. They continued on via Mount Bryan, Canowie Station, James-town, Mount Remarkable (Melrose), Stirling, and on to Willochra. There they met a wandering Central Australian native who spoke English quite fluently and behaved like a white man. He told them of the far-out land still hundreds of miles across desert waste. His intelligence encouraged the missionaries greatly, and they pushed steadily on past Hookina, Mundawanna, and Strangways Springs.

During November the heat became almost unbearable. Their lips cracked and bled. Swirling hot winds parched and shrivelled stock feed and blew it away in clouds of choking dust. A wagon split in two, and when repaired it tipped over and smashed precious supplies into the rock and sand. Known surface waters had dried up, and dry travel between more reliable waters was growing longer and longer. Stinking mud-holes, once filled with good water, were now death traps for weakened animals. The missionaries split into two lots, later into three travelling parties; and learnt the wisdom of slow travel sometimes at night. They had to return again and again over many miles for weak horses, cattle, and sheep left behind to rest. On 7 February 1876 they reported: 'We are stuck in sand, and are unable to continue, as our horses for the lack of water are too weak to pull.' One of the missionaries stripped and went to wash his tattered clothes in a precious mud puddle; on his return he discovered that all his clothes, which he had left to soak, had been trampled deep down into the mud by thirsty cattle.

Daily temperatures rose to 130 degrees in the sun. Tree-less gibber plains and desert lay before them. The promised land seemed ridiculous, unbelievable. Many of the sheep had to be left behind. Eleven hundred had died of thirst in one area where it had not rained for twelve months. Dingoes raided the sheep-fold at night, and followed openly by day to pull down any weakened sheep they could surround. The expedition straggled out in three different parts with two hundred miles between its lead and tail. It was undermanned, with food supplies running out, when Kempe and Schwarz had to call a halt, and wrote back by letter to Bethany: 'It is fearful, cruel, to travel in summertime.' Passing travellers, more experienced, less heavily equipped, unencumbered by stock, helped them again and again. Some of the letters and messages got through to Bethany. Pastor Heidenreich travelled up with horses to join the expedition, and on 14 May 1876 reported:

> I bought another 9 horses, we had two foals, making a total of 44. We lost through death 5 draught horses, 4 foals, 1 ran away, sold 3, with 31 on hand. Of cattle, 17 left. Bought 2 cows and 1 calf, also 6 oxen to pull waggons, making a total of 25. Twenty-three left on 14th May. Together, with lambs, 400 sheep. Five dogs, 4 hens, 1 rooster. Supplies: ¾ bag of flour, ¼ sugar.

A retreat to civilization could not be considered. Even though they had only four hundred sheep left of an original flock of three thousand one hundred, the missionaries were still convinced that they could battle on against odds that had turned back more experienced men.

On 29 May 1876 the expedition reached Dalhousie Springs, only to find the area overcrowded with three other parties travelling with stock. It was a desert outpost with the last reliable water for many miles; and northward travel had ceased. Further progress depended on good rainfall. It might fall within a week, possibly not for years. Pastor

Kempe set up an open-air blacksmith's shop to carry out urgent repairs, and also set up a crude wool-press. They shore the weakened sheep by hand and cleaned the wool and squeezed the fleece into rough bundles. Some day, perhaps, some of the wool might find its value in a city market and provide some small credit. Little did the missionaries know they were to stay eleven months before the drought was to break sufficiently to enable the full expedition to move on.

There were many days without a cloud in the sky; day after day when clouds formed in battalions and marched and rumbled away into hazy distance without a drop of rain falling. It was devastating mockery in a thirsty land, where rare floods sometimes bogged every yard of the earth's coloured surface. Nevertheless, on 28 June 1876, Pastor Kempe and Pastor Heidenreich, and one of the paid workers, left with an old dray and one riding horse between them, and travelled northwest to intercept the Finke River via Charlotte Waters. Cool winter days and nights helped them over a sixty-mile dry stretch. They continued up beside the great sandy bed of the Finke and turned north up the Hugh River to Owen Springs, in the known tracks of John McDouall Stuart. From Owen Springs they skirted below the red walls of the Waterhouse Range, crossed sandhill country westwards towards the Finke again, and camped about one mile north of the deep and colourful Finke Canyon, forty miles long, winding in its wild grandeur through the James and Krichauff Ranges.

This was the land of the broad valley, bounded by high ranges, where Surveyor-General Goyder had told them a Mission might be established. Beneath spreading river gums they said a simple prayer for guidance, and sank a shallow well in the dazzling white sand. The water was brackish, but they felt a growing confidence in the country they saw about them during twelve days spent in strenuous riding on the one saddle-horse, and walking turn about. The land was at its best. Rain had evidently fallen along the broad plain running east and west, now known as the Missionary Plain. The great Finke, a quarter of a mile wide, sandy and dry, wound down from the north-west across the plain. High driftwood indicated past flooding. Ernest Giles had ridden over the spot on Thursday, 5 September 1872. The deep-blue and red peaks of the Macdonnells stood out twenty miles northward, and all the unknown mystery of Giles's Krichauff plateau to southward. Central Australia turned on its best winter days, with sunlight gleaming through grass and spinifex, and the shadows of morning and evening deepening the incredible colour of the hills.

The sheep and cattle and valuable equipment were still more than three hundred miles back at Dalhousie. The drought would have to break over the intervening desert and reduce the distances between waters before the slow-travelling stock could be brought through. Kempe and Heidenreich quickly retraced their outward dray tracks back to Dalhousie, reaching there on 30 August 1876 with encouraging accounts of the country Goyder had recommended to them.

Supplies were now reduced to raisins and dried fruit, until someone in the Dalhousie community of waiting expeditions lent them fifty pounds of flour; but the position was desperate, and Pastor Kempe was forced to take horses and dray and travel nearly two hundred miles south to Peake for supplies.

The drought at Dalhousie broke during late summer, early in 1877; and on 9 April 1877 the full expedition moved forward at last, and made good and steady progress over country that had been barren and waterless, but that was now covered with green feed and good water. They arrived at the chosen spot on the eastern bank of the Finke River on 4 June 1877. There they immediately held a simple service of thanksgiving; and it is on record that they felt greatly strengthened in heart.

Their foundation flocks were sadly depleted, but the missionaries evidently had tremendous faith and belief that they soon would be a self-supporting community. They had brought many varieties of seeds to put in the ground. Several days' journey to eastward the new Overland Telegraph Line hummed its costly single strand north and south across the continent. It could convey an urgent message, but could not provide food or equipment. That had to come up over the long, slow desert and death route of a thousand miles.

Foundation during cool winter months was one thing; survival through the hot hell of summer was another. A new drought brought dysentery, scurvy, and fever; and semi-starvation on a heavy meat diet nearly crippled the merciful work time and time again. Early contact with wanderers of the primitive races they had come so far to help proved disappointing. These early missionaries were to discover by costly experience that Australia's inland desert nomad was the most improvident man on earth, belonging to a people who had never seen water boil, and had never tilled gardens, raised stock, or thought of the morrow; who went through terrible initiation tortures in youth as a hardening for manhood. Some tragic mistakes were made by the missionaries, mistakes that at the time might have seemed foolhardy, unwarranted perhaps, but that slowly set up a valuable store of experience and knowledge.

Their dreams of being a self-supporting community soon received a rude shock. Crops failed one after the other. Wheat, maize, barley, melons, pumpkins, vegetables, fruit, all were tried, and shot almost eagerly above the earth to sprout rapidly, only to wilt away in blazing heat and wind-driven sand. They made crude sledges and buckets of wood, and hauled and carted water from wells and soaks, and poured it into the ground.

Water! It mocked them. Each yard of rich sandy soil had strange fertility, ready to give forth tremendous plant-growth, but it thirsted for water. The damp patch on a summer evening of hard water-hauling was a steaming oven by morning, a dried-out bed of windblown sand and earthy powder by midday. Their small plants burnt off at ground level and rolled away with the hot winds. So they built bough shelters, and gardened beneath the shade. The results were a little better, but as summer heat killed much of their labour, so did the black frosts of bitter winter.

They named the settlement the Finke River Mission, and the area Hermannsburg, because of a strange, tiered red mountain in the Krichauff Range several miles south-ward, which reminded them of a place in their homeland. Paster Kempe took charge of the work, with Pastor Schwarz as assistant. The first white woman at Hermannsburg was Karoline Rosine Dorothea, the wife of Pastor Schwarz. She made the long thousand-mile journey across the desert; and their daughter, Wilhelmine Charlotte Dorothea, born on 19 March 1879, was the first white child born at that far-out, isolated place. Pastor Kempe travelled back to Dalhousie to meet his bride. They were married there in an old tattered tent on 1 March 1878, by the Reverend L. Schulze, and set out on a long and slow honeymoon journey on the open desert road.

The women brought a great deal of comfort, but for them the battle was tough and desperate, and household facilities primitive and rare in the extreme. They had the faith and devotion of saints, and rare courage, strengthened greatly, perhaps, by the almost unbelievable colours of the distant hills. Some of the short recorded comments and reports are graphic and filled with meaning:

> Dec. 1880:...Two years and six months without rain. Hard on our wives. Mostly meat diet....
>
> 20th January, 1881: Various plants and even trees growing nicely...the hot wind we have had for two months has dried off everything....

Two home-made windmills and a wooden pump helped a little; and a crude dam, dug by hand, 150 feet long, 20 feet wide, and 6 feet deep in the sand, caught and held a little water; but it was mostly a failure. Late in 1882:

> Plenty of vegetables now in winter. However, summer sun scorches everything....

2nd April, 1883: Gardening successful only if ground kept wet all the time. Watering with bucket not sufficient....

1886:...We have a garden of three acres full of vegetables, especially beans. First time harvested spuds....

April, 1887: Remunerative agriculture under present conditions impossible....

2nd January, 1890: Thermometer never under 112 for weeks. This heat has shrivelled everything....

Stock were drowned in rare floods; some wandered afield in the wake of misleading desert storms, and were speared and eaten by the men the missionaries had laboured so far to help. Outward mail and pleas for help and more seeds to sow, again and again, took many months to get to Bethany and back again; inward bullock-wagon and camel freight took up to two years to arrive, and cost up to £75 a ton. Years passed before the animal transport route was reduced from one thousand to eight hundred miles.

The missionaries burnt and made lime, hauled rocks from the Finke River bed, and built walls that are still standing firm and strong. They thatched the roofs first with grass in a clay compound. Summer flies carried sickness and spread eye blight. White ants worked silently at all the first wooden structures, until the missionaries found that it was wiser not to build with timber in contact with the ground.

In 1880 a man named Warburton founded the Glen Helen Cattle Station at the head of the Finke; and the Mission had a close neighbour, vaguely thirty miles away in the Macdonnell Ranges a little west of north through a long, red, and beautiful gorge of vertical and tilted rock walls, down through which the broad, tree-lined Finke emerged from its unknown source. Two small stone Mission buildings had been completed, and the natives were moving in, curious, begging, some sick and confused, a few in anger, defiant and troublesome. It seemed impossible to teach them anything useful, or to encourage them to adapt themselves to the slow but certain spread of civilization that would gradually disperse them and lure or drive them from their proven hunting grounds where existed the only balanced diet they knew how to get. The missionaries tried to understand and teach a primitive people who believed in witchcraft; who believed their ancestors were rocks, birds, animals; and who spent tremendous energy in vivid body-decorated chants and wild dancing to a weird legendry and mythology of the past.

Almost in desperation, and knowing not quite what to do, Kempe and Schwarz gradually taught the natives to sing Christian hymns; and found a strange and willing response and a glimmer of understanding in the melody of the white man.

In 1891 the Finke River Mission was nearly abandoned. Drought had ruined the land. Sickness, including dysentery and dread pneumonia, had followed drought; and the wells and waters of the Finke were salt and stinking. Pastor Schwarz had left with his family on 19 September 1889 on a long-overdue furlough, and had not returned. Pastor Kempe was an ageing, wasting man. On 13 November 1891 his wife died after having given birth to their sixth child. She was buried beside their son Paul, who had died on 22 December 1889, aged six years. On 26 November

1891, broken and dispirited, Kempe turned his back on the Mission and set out with four of the remaining children on the long journey southward. The infant child was left in the charge of another Mission worker. Months later, Kempe reached the south safely. He had once been a strong man; but sickness and worry had reduced him to seven stone in weight.

CHAPTER V
A PROBLEM IN HUMANITY

For several years after the tragic departure of the Reverend
F. A. H. Kemp from Hermannsburg, Mission work stood
practically at a standstill. A lay missionary, C. E. Eggers,
took over until the Reverend Mr Warber arrived in 1892
and left again in 1893. He was followed for another short
period by the Reverend L. Heidenreich and a Mr Kliche,
of Bethany, South Australia. A reform took place in the
control of the Mission. It came under the Immanuel Synod
of Lutherans, who sent a call of duty to the Reverend
Carl Strehlow in Germany. Once again an inexperienced
Missionary entered the land, to journey into a wilderness
that had conquered many good bushmen. Strehlow arrived
at the Finke River Mission, Hermannsburg, in October
1894, and felt the burning blast of a particularly hot
summer. He battled on for twenty-eight long years, and

placed on record the dialects and myths and legends of the Arunta (Arundta, Aranda) natives; learnt their customs, manners, and fervent inherited beliefs, until he became an understanding power among them. He alone could control and guide many of them. They had tremendous faith in him; but about him he saw the unmistakable signs of a dying race, now fugitive from civilization. The native needed vast space in his own domain, freedom, unlimited movement, and time to gather his own bush food and water so necessary to provide a diet that was instinctive to him, and as definite as the centuries. The country was far too poor to support large community groups, and thus most of the time they must hunt and collect bush foods in small groups or families. Every advance of the white settler interfered with known supplies of food and water. Gradually the bewildered remnants of once strong tribal units either moved into the nearest white settlements and lost their tribal beliefs in beggary, or turned to the Mission for help; but unhygienic congregation about the Mission soon eliminated natural greens and roots; and there was no immediate compensation.

It set up an appalling problem in humanity that has been understood by very few people.

Strehlow found the remnants of the once virile and proud Central Australian natives a filthy and sick people. They had recoiled from the shock of civilization. Some had gone in to white settlements. A few of them had been well treated. Many had been exploited. All had lost their tribal life, and most of them had become cunning paupers and beggars. Vice, prostitution, and disease followed. Yet some of the young native men proved good workers with stock, and thus became an important economic potential in the development of Central Australia. These young men had once been the hunters for the old and infirm; and the aged were now without support in their nomadic wanderings. Government ration depots supplied some of the wants of the aged, who in many instances shared or bartered all given to them and became surrounded by more detribalized paupers and beggars.

It was not a pretty story. It was not a new story.

Time and distance mocked Strehlow; but he slowly laid a permanent foundation for Christianity. His study and his extraordinary understanding of the native mind enabled him to choose and train native evangelists. These men wandered far afield, and explained to their tribesmen the Christian doctrine of the white man. In 1895 a South Australian man called Haemerling, assisted by native labourers, built the Mission church. It became a place of meeting. Natives travelled in over long distances to hear the white man who had learnt to speak to them in their own language. Today the church is far too small for the mixed congregation of black and white. Those who cannot crowd in sit outside in the loose sand beneath shady trees. Some still do not understand; but they like the singing.

Constant toil and repeated illness weakened Carl Strehlow through the years; still he battled on, deaf to all entreaties to rest awhile and seek medical attention; until pleurisy and dropsy forced him to leave Hermannsburg on a long journey by wagon down the rough and lonely mail track beside the Finke River. Mrs Strehlow and their son

Ted nursed him on a painful and difficult journey. It was October, the same month of blasting summer heat in which Strehlow had arrived at the Mission twenty-eight years before. They then had no one to help them, no magical radio, no merciful Flying Doctor Service; but about them the deep shadowy red of the great sandstone canyons beating back the terrible heat. A hundred miles from Hermannsburg Strehlow was in agony and unable to bear the terrible jolting. A native boy raced on to the Elliott family of the Horseshoe Bend of the Finke River for assistance.

The Reverend Carl Strehlow was buried at the Horseshoe on 21 October 1922 by Pastor Stolz, in a coffin made of flimsy old packing-cases. His passing was mourned by many, and his name in the centre of Australia was and always will be respected. His influence on the native problem and his research works and translations will continue to bear fruit for generations to come. His son, T. G. H. Strehlow, Lecturer in English Literature at Adelaide University, followed to some extent in his father's footsteps, and compiled valuable records of the traditions and habits of the Central Australian native, partly from the valuable records left by his father, and partly from his own lifelong experience, which included a span from 1936 until May 1942 as Patrol Officer and Deputy Director of Native Affairs at Alice Springs. His book, *Aranda Traditions*, is a very important addition to Australian knowledge.

Yet a third time a missionary was to travel from afar to enter a strange land. The Reverend F. A. H. Kempe had worked from 1875 until 1891; Carl Strehlow from 1894 until his death in 1922; and now, in 1926, the

Reverend F. W. Albrecht arrived from missionary studies in Germany, and learnt a great deal from Mr Heinrich, the Hermannsburg Mission schoolmaster, who had been sent up temporarily from Tanunda, South Australia.

With Albrecht's arrival another deadly drought set in and threatened the whole native population with extinction. Precious waters, usually reliable, gave out and narrowed down hunting areas. Hot winds blasted the earth once again and burnt irreplaceable herbs and roots. Infant mortality rose to eighty per cent. Adult natives could not resist illness, and commenced to die off in groups. Pastor Albrecht was promoted to Mission Superintendent in 1929, and quickly brought the drought-stricken plight of the natives to the notice of Government authorities, and requested medical help and advice to combat the scorbutic conditions sweeping through the native camps. Many of the natives had become almost completely dependent upon the white man's foods, and, quickly losing all desire for their own bush foods, found it easy to accept and beg for tea, sugar, white flour, and preserved meat. They had little alternative. Settlement and drought by now had split once-balanced tribal units into helpless minor groups.

The reports of medical men and scientists did not surprise the Reverend F. W. Albrecht. A great deal of valuable work was carried out by Professor C. B. Cleland, Professor Harvey Johnson, Dr H. K. Fry, and, later, Dr Charles Duiguid, all of Adelaide. It was obvious that the old aboriginal order of nomadic wandering and living could not be restored *in toto*. Memory of the white man could not be erased from the native mind. A transition was in force,

46

and more than normal strength was essential to weather it. Fresh fruits and vegetables were necessary to replace native plant foods, particularly for nursing mothers and growing children. Ordinary white flour was almost slow death when stuffed in quantity into native organs. Limited wild meat would have to be replaced at least partially by beef, mutton, and goat.

The missionaries followed the matter up with relentless energy. Somehow, crops had to be grown and greens provided on a scale larger than had ever been considered before, but a giant garden could not be grown overnight. Schwarz and Kempe had failed mostly in their heartbreaking early experiments. Water, the lack of it, and scorching sun in summer, were still the main problems. Meanwhile the scorbutic scourge was sapping all power of resistance from men, women, and children. To combat it in the urgency of time, large quantities of ordinary dried peas were donated from various sources, soaked in water till they sprouted, and the tender young green shoots given to the natives to eat. It was a simple ruse that succeeded greatly. Hundreds of cases of oranges were purchased, many of them donated, and transported by every available means from the new railhead at Alice Springs, and distributed to the bewildered natives.

An odd aspect of colour and wild natural beauty entered into the fight.

Watercolour artists were attracted to the red hills and coloured valleys of Central Australia. They gasped in amazement, painted many landscapes; and returned to the cities to talk and show their pictures of a strange land where vivid colour ran riot. Two of these artists, the Misses Una and Violet Teague, travelled from Melbourne to Hermannsburg. On their return to Melbourne they and others organized a relief fund to establish a reliable water-supply. Today Hermannsburg has its gravitated water system, dropping 117½ feet through 344 chains of cement pipe-line from the Kaporilya (Kaparulja) Springs of 10,000 to 13,000 gallons daily flow into a main storage tank of 47,000-gallon capacity, at the Mission Station. The Melbourne artists and the public made the money possible; Surveyor Blatchford of Perth and Edgar Horwood of Adelaide ran the heights and levels down a wild rocky gorge, through sandhill after sandhill, and across the wide Finke River of sand and rare floods; Arthur Latz and six natives started digging with hand tools and pipe-laying in the sapping heat of 5 December 1934. On an average, eight natives assisted throughout the job, and nearly a year later, on 1 October 1935, clear spring water gravitated from an odd crack in a giant sandstone slab in the red Krichauff hills, out over the spinifex plains and shifting sandhills, beneath the sand and rock of the broad river, and flowed out at Hermannsburg, sixty years after Kempe and Schwarz had set out on their long, almost tragic journey to save a vanishing race.

Was it now too late?

It was an unforgettable event of great importance; a flow of sparkling water with a gleam of light and hope.

There is a very large vegetable garden now, tended by many native women. They are rightly proud of giant cauliflowers, lettuce, kohlrabi, carrots, large and juicy red beetroot, parsnips, clean large tomatoes, marrows, and even onions – grown in sand, thirsty, loose sand, feet deep. The daily vegetable requirements are large and increasing. Each picturesque old stone house occupied by the Mission staff boasts its own vegetable and flower garden, orange-trees, and small square of precious lawn. Water is laid throughout; heavy brush and wire-netting fences keep out plundering camels, goats, donkeys, horses, cows, dingoes, and native hunting dogs – so starved by their dusky owners to encourage them to hunt, that they will raid and eat anything soft enough to chew.

The large vegetable garden is a vivid-green oasis in a sandy waste. It consumes thousands of gallons of water daily, particularly in summer, when broiling heat and dry winds still parch many of the plants. To the casual visitor it is just a very large chequerboard of smaller gardens in the sand to one side of the Mission, west of where drifting sand has piled over the old cemetery wall; but to the missionaries and the natives it is practical salvation, and the barometer by which all health is judged and maintained.

At last the rot of scurvy was stamped slowly out, and the scales balanced again between life and death, survival and extinction. Missionaries, scientists, artists, and many other helpers had not failed. Government financial assistance, time and time again, had been liberal and quickly available. Since 1935, births have exceeded deaths and children are healthy. More than one thousand of the Northern Territory's fourteen thousand natives may be found within the scope of Hermannsburg and its distant outposts at Areyonga and Haast's Bluff.

River gum in the Ormiston River bed, a mile before the Ormiston River emerges from its deep canyon through the Macdonnell Ranges. The distant rocks are a brilliant red with purple shadows.

Large pool and bright-red cliffs with nesting shags at the beginning
of the Ormiston Gorge, Macdonnell Ranges.

Many of the older natives still showed weakness and inability to resist sickness. Tuberculosis claimed a number of them in the aftermath of the scurvy period, which ran from 1926 to 1930, when the disastrous drought terminated with a flood.

Superintendent Albrecht felt that the natives must be taught more industry and responsibility; and somehow, the tendency of more than ninety per cent to loaf at the fringe of civilization had to be overcome. It seemed a tragic waste of time, useless, and the forerunner of slow moral and physical death, merely to feed and clothe and preach Christian salvation to the unfortunate remnants of a nomadic race, unless the extremely difficult and important task of instilling at least a token measure of ambition was tackled also.

Thousands of years of wandering stripped the Central Australian aboriginal of independent ability to plan a future, and made him master only of the moment. His dwellings always have been temporary crude things of sticks and leaves and grass, built in a few hours and abandoned at the mystic call of far-away food, water, or tribal ceremony. He gorged himself today, starved tomorrow, and shared his temporary possessions. He believed in his descent from spirit and dream forms of totemic ancestors in an amazingly intricate and ceremonial network, which still baffles many of the world's foremost anthropologists. A curiously talented race, with the minds of designing mathematicians yet little ability to count; whose great strength and past lay back in the ages of legend and decorative ceremony; whose future was never their own concern, but the pawn of circumstance; a people who could not think ahead, but feverishly worshipped the traditions of the past.

Time has now proved the location choice of Hermannsburg by the pioneers Kempe and Schwarz in 1877, to be a fortunate one, for the main administrative centre now stands in relation to the outposts at Areyonga and Haast's Bluff as a buffer between the civilized areas of Alice Springs and the far-out wilderness lands stretching beyond the Western Australian border; and the native may wander fully as his ancestors wandered, or turn to the Mission for help when he needs it.

But he must work when under Mission jurisdiction, for which he will learn the benefits and curses of money, what money stands for, and what he may purchase with it for his own good. At far-out Haast's Bluff, and at Areyonga, with unoccupied desert for hundreds of miles to westward, these remnant people may now wander in and cash their desert trophies of dingo scalps and animal skins and hides for many of the comforts of civilization.

Disappointments, misjudgments, and some thankless treachery, at first were many; but one by one, industries have been established, and the inherent laziness is being slowly reduced. The natives have been taught to skin the kangaroos and euros they spear when hunting far out, and to exchange the skins for money. They have been taught to tan the skins, make harness, boots, shoes, rugs, useful aprons and bags. They may use modern machinery at Hermannsburg or work by hand far afield. Men who prove themselves capable and trustworthy with camels, horses, or cattle are given an opportunity to acquire a small herd of cattle under the control of a Board on which they have adequate representation. Known as 'Native Pastoralists', they graze their small herds far out at little-known waters and in hidden grassland valleys over the vast Aboriginal Reserve that is theirs to the exclusion of all white men other than missionaries and Native Affairs Patrol Officers. The Government has given strong encouragement by putting down a series of bores in distant places where grazing would otherwise be impossible.

Now and then a small mob of bullocks will be sold either through the Mission or to the Department of Native Affairs. Conditions are strict but fair. The way is wide open for a man who shows ambition; and late in 1948, none of the pastoralists was in debt.

Many of the native women do embroidery and rug work, which is sold through the Mission; but perhaps the most unusual industry that has been established is the Watercolour Art School, the prodigy of Rex Battarbee. Some of the students are already famous; others well on the road.

Battarbee was born at Warrnambool, Victoria, in 1895, and was badly wounded in the first world war. After a very slow recovery he commenced to paint in water-colours; and in 1928 he set out with a fellow artist, John Gardner, on a motor-caravan tour that eventually led them to the colourful hills of the Macdonnell Ranges. In 1934 Battarbee won a Commonwealth prize for the best water-colour of the year, and in that year he held an exhibition of his locally painted pictures at Hermannsburg Mission. It created extraordinary interest among the natives, and brought forth a frank request to the Reverend F. W. Albrecht by a full-blooded native, Albert Namatjira, that he be given an opportunity to put colours on paper just as the white man had done. Albert Namatjira's request could not be overlooked. He had always been a conscientious worker, with more than average intelligence, and had spent most of his life in the colourful hill country round Hermannsburg since his birth on 28 July 1902.

In 1936 Rex Battarbee returned to Hermannsburg and found Albert waiting eagerly for him with striking examples of decorative colouring on paper and wood. Battarbee taught the aboriginal the technique of drawing and the use of colours for a short period of two months, and then stood by to watch an amazing progress that resulted in an exhibition of forty-one of Albert Namatjira's paintings in Melbourne, late in 1938. They were all sold.

For Albert it was only the beginning. He has since held several exhibitions, and his pictures have gone overseas. He has no desire to see the capital cities where his exhibitions are held. Rex Battarbee believed that the trait of artistic expression was dormant within many of the natives, handed down through centuries of rock artists and body decorators, whose crudely expressive paintings are on the walls of many caves and cliffs; thus in Central Australia, the badly wounded soldier of the first world war also found his own future.

Battarbee's Hermannsburg Art School is now a paradox. His pupils are individualists, not copyists, each one steadily developing a style; one bold in colour; one heavy in outline, another with extraordinary delicacy; all with astonishing perspective, and all linked by a recognizable aboriginal quality that always will be beyond the white man. In this the aboriginal painters are unique. Battarbee has given his services voluntarily and without stint in creating one of the most important Art movements in the world. Not only does it open up a new field for an ambitious native with more than normal talent, but it is building up an extensive and permanent record in colour of Central Australia. Three of the paintings are in the possession of Her Royal Highness Princess Elizabeth. Albert Namatjira has now been equalled, if not surpassed, by the brothers Otto and Edwin Pareroultja; while others who are progressing rapidly include Oskar Namatjira, Enos Namatjira, Reuben Pareroultja, Richard Moketarindja, Henock Raberaba, Walter Ebatarindja, and Russel.

And Battarbee? The master is now shoulder to shoulder with some of his own pupils, who are devoted to him. Few men have done more in life towards a common good.

While the Reverend Mr Albrecht told me the strange story of Hermannsburg, clouds blew up from the southwest and blotted out the deep red of the James and Krichauff Ranges, and a bitter cold winter rain settled in, swirled like ice through the stone-floored, gauzed verandas, and sent many natives to shelter round small campfires. There was some commotion outside, and the news came that Albert Namatjira had just arrived 'in' from a painting walkabout of the Palm Valley of the Finke, in the little-known wilderness canyons of the Krichauff Range. He would be going out again within a few days; but he had brought with him nearly fifty watercolours for display and selection that night before the Board of Management of the Hermannsburg Art Council.

CHAPTER VI
VOICE OF THE AGES

Twenty miles along the Alice Springs track, Pastor Albrecht dropped me, fully laden with food for several days, and water-bottles that might last twenty-four hours. He continued on through the scattered mulga, without any lights on the big truck, towards Alice Springs; thence to continue to Henbury Station to christen a native child. To Albrecht, an all-night drive after a day of hard work was merely an incident in a constant battle against time. In an hour of skilful driving through moonlight, this amazing disciple had told me quietly of his boyhood wish to be a missionary.

For a while I stood alone, unaware of the freezing cold, and knew that no words of mine could ever express adequately my admiration for this man, Albrecht, and his helpers. Time and fatigue, disappointment and hardship meant little. Their goal was selfless, and far beyond the understanding of ordinary man.

The noise of the truck died away, and I walked quietly on in the brilliant moonlight. Ten miles northward the Macdonnells ran at right angles, mysterious and rugged, and bathed now in a liquid white-gold that made the blues and reds of the day seem as an event of another age and place. I could hear the bellowing of cattle being held 'on camp' by native stockmen about three miles to the north. Albrecht had suggested that I walk out and camp with them; but I was fresh and eager to go, and turned away to the north-west, across clay-pans and stony ridge country, with mulgas and ironwoods scattered thinly and shimmering like silver; and vivid white river gums lining small, dry, sandy watercourses that all headed southward from the ranges. I headed through that brilliant golden night towards the Ellery River. I was not tied to camel pads and could set a line to any distant point and travel on towards it over country too rough to be penetrated by any other means.

By the following evening I had walked nearly forty miles, most of it up and beside hot, sandy river bed, through and round unbelievable rock terraces, razor-backs, and curved and exposed strata piled up and down in mammoth switchback formation, hundreds of feet high and hundreds of feet down.

Natives claim that a tremendous snake once slithered out of the west, heading towards the east, with long patterned body curved up and down along the ground. Its head was many miles away towards the rising sun, ready to devour an unfortunate victim, when it was turned to stone. The simile was easy to recognize.

The temperature rose to eighty-nine degrees shortly after midday. That first midwinter daylight walk was a tough, tiring one; and my heavy walking shoes split and pulled apart over the sharp, abrasive rocks.

The purple cliffs of the chilly morning, fantastic in delicate light and shade, mysterious and intriguing, were red walls radiating heat at midday, and I had to narrow my eyes to slits beneath a wide-brimmed hat; but, in the evening of that incredibly warm winter day, the closed valleys freshened to a steady breeze, and the soft shadows of the hills returned at sunset to darken slowly beneath the dusk.

I camped at Ellery* Gap, where the river has cut through one of the main ranges, down and down through millions of years of time and hundreds of feet of red rock, until now this gateway through the mountain is nine hundred feet deep, a few yards wide, and about a quarter of a mile long. A deep, ice-cold pool fills the gap. You must swim through its gloomy depths or climb high over steep cliff and massive rubble. A loud whisper or cough echoes into startling return from wall to wall; and birds and bats whistle through night and day. Animals approach furtively to drink. Natives often camp well back from it, although it once was a favourite meeting-place and ceremonial ground of tribal wanderers. Every gash and cave in the hills, and every high rocky point, carries a myth or legend of the time

---

* Udepata.

when they lived as birds or animals, reptiles, or ancestral tribal forefathers in the 'dreamtime' of long, long ago.

Many curved strata rise up beneath the cavernous right or eastern wall to an inaccessible ledge, crag, and bluff. There were shrieks and calls of birds beyond vision; hawks and shags in noisy conflict. The wild grandeur was marred only by prominent white signwriting on the red rock:

'KATHNER-HOPE CAMP, NOVEMBER 1945.'

The Ellery River, tributary of the Finke, was named in memory of the astronomer Ellery by the Central Australian explorer Ernest Giles, on Monday, 2 September 1872.

At dusk I stripped to swim. The air was dry and warm; but the water, now dark and treacherous, was too cold to risk alone, and I splashed awhile, noisily, at its edge, conscious of the hollow echoes. Towards midnight a far-off whispering came in over the high hills. At first it was a complete sound in itself, distant and soft, then gradually becoming powerful and definite. It was soon part of the whole wilderness: part of the pines and ghost gums, and cycads and spinifex, and of the rocks and hills and valleys; surely the voice of an ancient people dreaming, and yet stirring once again in an ancient land; the ghosts of millions down the ages. It increased in volume from its first steady whisper, then it rose to a rushing by of all life and death, coming from afar, and going – goodness only knows where. In the vacuum of utter stillness beside a dying fire, I could sense acutely the first aborigines peering into darkness and fearfully chanting the legends of mythology that are now in danger of being lost for ever.

It continued for two or three hours until I realized that a boisterous breeze had descended to ground level with a penetrating chill that sent me into the depths of my sleeping-bag to shiver until morning.

Next day I climbed the high, bare quartzite ridge west of the gap, up through prickly spinifex and rocky outcrop, to the crest one thousand feet up; and looked out through winter's clear visibility over this strangely beautiful coloured land of parallel ranges both north and south; for I was in the middle of them all. Some curved in scalloped crests running from west to east; other ranges, particularly to northward, towered higher than where I stood, in mitred peaks of deep purple, vivid blue, and shadowy red. Forty-two of these mitred peaks stood up on the northern range. Slightly east of north, about ten miles away, a dark slit of unfathomable shadow bit deeply into the rock. It was not shown on my maps, which indicated very little; but it is known to a few as Connann's Gorge. A rugged mountain with three towering eastern buttresses, marked as Mount Giles, and more spectacular by far than all the rest, blocked a valley to the north-west – a hidden monument to an Australian explorer.

The long walk back to Hermannsburg was cooler and more pleasant than the first hot day. Water was scarce, with only one good pool thirty yards long, and several stinking rock-holes. Approach to these putrid holes was heralded by hundreds of parrots, pigeons, finches, hawks, crows, apostle-birds, butcher-birds, wrens, and common chats, all of deep interest to ornithologists. I sighted Mount Hermannsburg's squared mass nearly twenty-five miles distant, and headed for it through scattered mulga and ironwood, and cut the Hermannsburg to Alice Springs track near the landing field.

There was to be a Sunday night singsong in the sandy yard beside the Superintendent's house. Rex Battarbee and I stood awhile beneath a starry night in the shadow of the tall river gums surrounding the Mission chapel. Dark figures were moving silently across; all church services for the day were over, and the spell of day was still upon the natives. More than a hundred had gathered in groups of about ten or fifteen round small fires. There was a loud buzz of chattering, subdued giggling and laughter, and the white of flashing eyes; and that strange heavy odour of the aboriginal. The missionaries and the visiting members of the Mission Board were seated back in shadow. Old Abel the full-blood leader of the community, stood up alone above all the others as they sat watching him, waiting for movement, and a little fearful of him. Abel is a sort of boss cocky, leader of the native evangelists, bell-ringer in chief, organizer and community foreman. In the darkness his snow-white hair and bristling white moustache almost hid a face darker than the night. He coughed and rattled an order in Arunta. There was immediate silence. He raised his hands, called for close attention, and made an announcement that had obvious reference to the white visitors.

I sat with Rex Battarbee and Pastor Albrecht. Then Abel moved right into the glow, raised his hands again for complete silence, and the band of a hundred or more native voices commenced to sing in deep rich harmony, clear as an organ. They sang in the Arunta language, then in English; and by far the loveliest and deepest effect, which revealed the unforgettable harmony and ease of control and exhilaration in their voices, came from the rendition by these stone-age, primitive people of the hymns of Christianity translated by the early missionaries. They have been singing since the first Central Australian missionaries, Pastors Schwarz and Kempe, knew not what else to teach them away back in 1877. One can imagine the patience of the teachers, and the bewilderment of the black man trying to judge and understand the strange new music of the voices brought by the white men; but the black man has been chanting his own beliefs down through the ages, in peace and passion. It is one of the instinctive things of life with him, linked with all ceremony, decoration, and fantasy.

I did not sleep well that night, but lay awake in the white, plastered, stone visitor's room at the eastern end of Arthur Latz's home. A late moon came in and played strange tricks on Battarbee's paintings round the walls. He slept like a log, unconscious of the hundred native voices I could not forget. I could sense the tragic passing of the native chants and ceremonies handed down with amazing accuracy and religious fervour by the patriarchal tribal elders, from generation to generation; only to be threatened with oblivion and forgetfulness.

But the savage and primitive ceremonies, once so much a part of the chanting, are now no more. White man's laws have condemned them; and slowly, through the period of bewilderment and transition, the native has replaced many of his chants and myths and legends with the hymns of the missionaries. It is because of all this that the research work of T. G. H. Strehlow, in the compilation of Aranda myths and legends, is an important addition to the history and traditions of Australia.

Pastor Gross brought out the big three-ton truck, loaded it with a large tucker-box, mattresses, seats, and cushions.

'All aboard! We're off to Palm Valley!' and almost immediately the truck was filled with Mission Board members and with native women of the domestic staffs. They clambered over the back and sides, passed up children, dumped them in corners or nursed them. 'Mo'-car ride' is always a treat, reserved as a reward for good work; and Mission trucks seldom travel without a few extras to help 'hold the road'.

The high plateau of millions of years ago extended over a vast area, and sloped southward. Deep down, hundreds and perhaps thousands of feet down, hidden cores and splines of harder rock ran east and west; and all the water-courses followed the natural slope and ran off southward.

Ages of slow erosion have worn the great plateau or plateaux down and the rivers, too, have dropped slowly, mostly keeping their original courses; and as the hidden splines became exposed, the rivers cut down through them at right angles. The Finke is the greatest of all these rivers. Twenty miles north-west of Hermannsburg Mission it emerges as one wide united watercourse from the Glen Helen Gorge of two miles of red-walled canyons. North of that again, ten and twenty miles, its radiating tributaries, the Pioneer, Ormiston, Redbank, and Davenport, emerge from crevice and canyon far beyond the way of the average traveller.

Off we went with our chattering, singing load, accompanied by a procession of dogs, a few hundred yards as far as the main channel of the Finke; skinny hunting dogs, pet dogs with superior air, mangy dogs, fat dogs huffing and whimpering, mongrel dogs and half-bred dingoes; all sorts of dogs, for the dog is Priority Number One hunting aid and flea-infested hot-water bottle on winter nights.

South of Hermannsburg the Finke sweeps wide and vivid white with clean sand, grandly and in magnificent colour contrasts with the red walls of the James Range; then it continues through forty miles of deep canyons separating the James to eastward from the wilder Krichauff hills to westward.

Palm Valley is a tributary ten miles down the Finke from Hermannsburg. The sandy road at first follows the bed of the Finke, and where the way is not sandy it is rocky and rough. We turned westward from the river, up a rocky watercourse that shook us all and brought yells of delight from the women. Pastor Gross deviated towards the massive red and purple walls of the Amphitheatre, rising and circling in gallery upon gallery of sandstone and shadow, with angry clouds now drifting overhead to give power to the whole scene. Out on the flat floor of the Amphitheatre a sandstone sphinx rises high and looks into the west; and well to southward a curving razorback, resembling the trunk of an elephant, juts out some hundreds of yards across the valley.

Pastor Gross drove cautiously over sharp rock into

Palm Valley itself, and stopped the truck on a flat red sandstone floor between red walls rising several hundred feet in shadowy galleries. Vivid-white ghost gums grew in high cracks, and glistening green cycad palms lined the northern walls. We scrambled from the truck and walked beside the stream running through an avenue of the rare *Livistona Mariae* palm, first seen and noted by Ernest Giles at a spot a few miles lower down the Finke, on Saturday, 3 August 1872. There were bulrushes in the pools, and small fish, and the native women soon squatted in a sandy patch to dig for small edible yelka bulbs. The area is a Scenic Reserve, but unpoliced; and visitors, in ignorance or selfishness, take the young palms in a vain attempt to grow them in city fern-houses. The trade is not great yet, but it will grow if it is not checked by flawless regulations. There is a big danger in this creeping sort of vandalism.

The Mission Board members wanted to surprise Albert Namatjira in his native haunts. His presence somewhere in the valley was known, but no smoke or track or sound betrayed his actual whereabouts. Possibly he was asleep somewhere beneath a tree, or on a distant crag painting another of his famous watercolours, or away hunting for lizards over distant hills; but here, somewhere, wandered an unspoilt man of nature, putting on record the colours of Central Australia. It was a paradox almost unbelievable.

CHAPTER VII
HEADWATERS OF
THE MIGHTY FINKE

The Reverend F. W. Albrecht suggested that I should go with the Board Members on another inspection by truck, as far as Glen Helen Gorge on the upper Finke. We set out with stockman Arthur Latz at the wheel; and Abel, once again organizing songs amongst the dozen native women riding in the back of the truck. Rex Battarbee and I sat above the cabin and faced the full force of the wind. We called at a large earthen dam, empty and dry. The missionaries shook their heads. The water position was acute, and expensive attempts to store water out in the 'sandhill' country had been so far a failure. Abel wandered about the top of the dam. He was amused. His white moustache and floppy old hat lent him some distinction.

'Long time ago,' he ventured – and waved a hand to

indicate vast country – 'this country he got plenty rain – but no dam. Now we got plenty dam – no rain. Mad place altogether.'

We drove north-east back towards the Finke, mile after mile over spinifex and sand and clay-pan dotted with monotonous mulgas. Battarbee pointed out Gosse's Range, a hazy pink massive crown of rock low down to the west, a vivid diadem of the desert. He explained that it was one thousand feet high, several miles across and perfectly round, hollowed in the centre, and well worth a visit. It was first visited by Ernest Giles on Sunday, 8 September 1872, and named in honour of Harry Gosse, one of the earliest officers attached to the original Alice Springs Overland Telegraph Station.

I was beginning to beware of distance and its treachery. Landmarks of the morning indicating only a few hours' journey to reach them, after a hard day of travel still could be distant landmarks of the evening.

Arthur Latz drove with great skill. He knew every rock, blade of grass, clump of spinifex, and gully. He knew the speed and momentum necessary to coax the truck over dry sandy watercourses that were certain traps for the inexperienced. We crossed the wide, dry bed of the Finke and spread a large picnic lunch in the sand. Latz grilled several pounds of fillet steak, and the women produced green salads grown in the sand of the Hermannsburg gardens. The missionaries offered simple grace to the music of crows overhead. Latz was worried about the water problem. He might have to collect all his native stockmen and shift the few cattle in a hurry – the problem was, where to? Drought was rearing its ugly head, to strike once again and undo years of patient shepherding and hard work.

After lunch we drove on into the north beside the east bank of the Finke, a few miles up into the foothills of the Macdonnells, and stopped at the track's end on solid rock strata. Battarbee and I walked ahead beside the river and in the shadow of its enclosing red cliffs. The rising strata had forced the water, which had trickled for miles deep beneath the sand, up to the surface, and there was an impressive chain of pools. Battarbee viewed everything with the eye of an artist, and was obviously planning a field programme for his class of native artists. I looked for camera shots and found plenty. He told me not to miss Ormiston Gorge, the far-flung, upper right-hand tributary of the Finke. He promised more colour and rocky grandeur there than anywhere else within a hundred miles of Alice Springs. Ormiston Gorge lies a fraction north of dead west, seventy-five miles by airline from Alice Springs, in a mountain maze where the parallel ridges of the Macdonnell Ranges system jump out of line awhile, and merge together near Mount Giles.

We missed Bryan Bowman, owner of the old Glen Helen Cattle Station, by a matter of two or three minutes. I had previously written to him and sent stores to await my arrival. Battarbee and I climbed several hundred feet up the rocky bluff west of the main gap, and looked down on the winding river and the silent old homestead and its broken windmill, less than a quarter of a mile away. We heard the faint whine of an engine and saw a long spurting trail of dust to north-west – Bowman, on his motor-bike, setting out possibly for days or weeks. This wizard has pitted

ABOVE: The crest of Mount Sonder, one of the red rock masses
rising close to five thousand feet above sea level at the western
end of the Macdonnell Ranges system.

BELOW: The eastern end of the red Wulpa (Walpa, Walpina) Chasm,
Mount Olga. The bluff on the left rises fourteen hundred feet.

Vertical rock strata above the sandy bed of the Finke at Glen Helen, Macdonnell Ranges. Note the cow at the left base for comparison.

himself and his bike against weather and distance in fertile land and desert sand; and apparently he goes when and where he wishes.

We sat awhile in late afternoon and traced the Finke winding away to north-west towards Mount Sonder* towering majestically four thousand eight hundred feet about fifteen miles away; then Battarbee pointed out the zigzag of the deep-green trees lining the Ormiston, junctioning with the Finke two or three miles to the north. In the distance, perhaps ten miles north-east, there was a rugged tangle of red cliffs, surmounted by spinifex-capped domes that indicated the only clue to where the twisting Ormiston might pierce the formidable barrier.

The missionaries and Battarbee, and Abel and his singers, returned to Hermannsburg, leaving me alone to watch the deep red and purple shadows of a Glen Helen evening turn the hills to fire, before a few minutes of deepening blue gave way to darkness and a bright starry night.

When camping right out in the open there is time and leisure to think of many things while the bowl of night turns slowly over. The freedom of thought and feeling is tremendous and lasting. I stored surplus gear in Bowman's old stone homestead and set off on foot before sunrise for Ormiston Gorge. The floor of the Finke Valley north-east of Glen Helen could have been the surface of the moon. The land seemed unreal, still and strangely silent except for the ventriloquial bell-note of a bird, striking like a distant,

* Named after Dr Will Sonder.

elusive, metallic hammer. Walls of red and brown rock ran east and west, rising and falling in curving razorbacks. There were stone figures, spires, slits, and caves in the walls, and the suggestion of prehistoric creatures behind each corner.

Even though it was midwinter, with a night temperature of twenty-nine degrees, the day was warm enough. Walking would be suicidal lunacy in summer. I crossed the Ormiston near the crumbling foundation of Ragget's old homestead. Ragget was a Glen Helen pioneer, and eventually retired to Alice Springs. There was a long, stinking pool in the river, which bent back and away from my destination. I took a short cut over rough hills far too rocky for camels. It was hard going, strenuous, and with the stabbing needles of the spinifex 'porcupine'-bush, piercing trouser leg, sock, and shoe; but the magnificent views from each crest were worth the effort. They enabled me to keep a check on the erratic course of the river, now making towards a point ahead of me from its long leg to eastward; but there still was no obvious way through the magnificent red barrier of rock, rising steadily higher and higher, as I approached, in an immense grandeur and depth of vivid colour.

Perhaps a mile from the barrier I entered the dry bed of the river at a point where it continued in an impressive strait for the cliffs. It was about seventy yards wide, with clean white sand and gravel between lines of tall, leaning river gums. An artist would find a picture in every tree.

I laboured slowly over the sand. Some of it was hardened like cement, but much of it was fine and soft and heavy going. It was not until I was within a hundred yards of a cavernous bluff rising against a much higher background of red rock and cliff, that I sensed water ahead and a probable bending of the river sharply to the right. Birds called louder than usual in this echoing place. It was a haunting, mysterious, noisy wilderness of red and purple shadows. I had seen the colours of the Ellery River twenty miles east of me, and of Palm Valley perhaps forty miles to the south. I had seen them at sunrise and sunset; and I had seen the sun set over Gosse's Range like a blood-red glowing jewel on a far plain; but the colours and shadows of the Ormiston have their own incredible power and depth. The sun had gone to northward in its winter arc of noon, behind the main range, and I had before me, rising up, a depth within depth of coloured shadow in every shade of purple, pink, and red; and deep in the shadows, perhaps half a mile away, the dim red walls of the main mountain rose high, terrace upon terrace, until the last precipice went up for hundreds of feet. The contrast between deep shadow and gleaming sunlight above the crest was so sudden that the northern hilltops directly in the path of the hidden sun seemed to be on fire.

Behind me, the lower and southern wall of the gorge was not so high; but it received the full force of the sun striking on its deep, rich red, and probably caused much of the coloured shadows and light beams by reflection. I scrambled cautiously beside a large sandbank above a long and deep pool that was patterned with delicate tracery from overhanging trees. On the opposite cliffs were many noisy shags, and some young screeching in large nests of twigs on small ledges; ducks swam in and out of a cave and quacked up an emphatic protest. Bright mulga and ringneck parrots flew up and down stream, and a whole convoy of busy budgerigars passed by in characteristic wavering flight, swiftly, noisily, up the gorge and beyond sight. Rock pigeons paraded like soldiers over the red rocks in the sun to my right. They moved oddly, in groups, several at a time – a quick run, stop, run; birds at drill. The whole place was now alive with movement.

Rex Battarbee had been right. Here was natural colour beyond description. It was high up in the sky, with shades of blue and mauve reflected from the cliffs. It was in the patches of green spinifex, clinging in pin-heads on the rubble slopes. It was in the water, the sand, even in the trees; and perhaps the slow-moving deep shadows were more colourful and mysterious than anything else. The colour was in the water-worn rocks of the river bed. There were boulders and slabs of green, grey, mauve, pink, white, red, black, and all the shades between. This colour system was entirely different to the bright colours of the canyon walls. It was of shades and tints, and went up about ten feet to normal flood level, proving that the basic colour of red was gradually being washed out of all rocks crashing from above. Rex Battarbee had told me of two other places that might equal the Ormiston – Central Mount Wedge, to northward of the Macdonnells, and King's Canyon, far off the beaten track in the western end of the George Gill Range. He had not been there, but Bryan Bowman had told him of it.

Some day, perhaps, I might see one or both of them!

There were plant-growth and small fish deep in the

71

pools, similar to the marine coral gardens of the Barrier Reef; and each pool had its own tinge of reflected colour. The running water continued for half a mile, during which the narrow gorge bent twice, sharply. Each bend was a spectacular overlapping of red cliff from left and right, giving a distant impression of inaccessibility, yet the scramble from boulder to boulder was easy and pleasant. There were no other human tracks. Euro, rock wallaby, and dingo tracks were plentiful. High up beneath the northern overhang, rattling stones indicated a startled euro climbing the almost perpendicular slopes and shelves with amazing speed. Brother to the kangaroo, the bulky euro can ascend mountain-sides with amazing agility.

The spring water was deep, ice cold, and sweet. There was no refuse, no rotting carcasses; and no exploring tourist had painted his name in white against the red. The place was alive with bird and animal life and colour, and death seemed to play no part in it.

Eventually I turned back and walked slowly down the gorge through deeper shadows than those of the morning, and through a deeper mystery of colour. A chilliness was sweeping down. The birds were less noisy. The change of light and my change of direction threw into ghostly relief many rock needles and spires jutting up towards stronger light.

A day later I was twenty miles west of the Ormiston, in the Redbank* tributary of the Finke. It is reputedly difficult of access; and, according to one account, emerges from a

---

* Oorachilpilla.

slit in the side of Mount Sonder nine hundred feet deep and three feet wide.

I did not find that nine-hundred-foot slit. Instead, I found a gloomy crevice a few feet wide, and no more than two hundred feet deep. The place was silent and dull, with one lonely duck dodging uncertainly in the shadowed water beneath a jagged overhang. The pool stank of cattle and manure. Their long track in to water led up over the rocky bed of the Redbank. I scrambled to the right, eastward and up above the crevice, and surprised a parade-ground of euros sunning themselves on rock terraces. They hopped off, mostly to northward. Then I went slowly on up Mount Sonder* to overlook all the tributaries of the Finke. It has been written more than once that Sonder is unscalable; and others have written of hardship in approach and ascent. The only hardship I experienced was the physical effort of walking up a long, exposed ridge of rock that cut my shoes badly. The rock is rough and abrasive, and the action of goose-stepping over the sharp spinifex is rough on clothes and shoes alike.

But to rise nearly two thousand eight hundred feet above the plateau of Central Australia, which is itself two thousand feet above sea level, is like rising above a prehistoric world before animal and human life existed. It was a crystal-clear day and, as my horizon widened, every shape of hill and mountain jutted up. All the watercourses were drawn neatly on a vast coloured canvas. To westward, the massive domes of Mount Zeil†, Razorback, and distant

---

* Oorich-ip-ma.
† Wallatrika.

Heughlin and Haast's Bluff well out on the horizon, were a filmy blue, etched in stereoscopic effect against a white sky faintly tinted with purple. To northward, range beyond range and isolated peak after peak rose up to confound any attempt to locate them on my maps, which I had already proved to be inaccurate and incomplete. A little east of south the red terraces of Mount Hermannsburg indicated the Mission forty miles away; and behind it all rose the green spinifex tops of the Krichauff and James Ranges.

It took a lively hour to climb Sonder. I found a cairn of stones that contradicted any report that the mountain had never been climbed. I looked down over dizzy, sharp, red razorbacks facing the east, and separated by canyons slashing down for many hundreds of feet. Even from the east, Sonder would be scalable by experienced climbers who know how to avoid masses of cracked, treacherous, overhanging rocks likely to crash outward and down.

A wedge-tailed eagle flew up over the side, swerved sharply at close sight of me, and vol-planed down into the eastern pound at terrific speed. Wildflowers were plentiful; the main one, a mauve bottle-brush, dominated the crests. To eastward the wilderness of the Macdonnells continued on towards Alice Springs in the parallel formation that seemed never-ending but not monotonous. About ten miles ahead, a large valley was blocked by the sharp walls of a pink and brown mountain, with its bare, crumbling sides also slashed with ravines. It was hard to pin this vivid panorama of mountains and valleys and distant fertile plains on to the accepted belief of barren, waterless, and monotonous desert waste. Undoubtedly it was wintertime, and I had to accept the testimony of others of its colour in summer mornings and evenings; but in summer the bare rock walls and closed valleys would radiate terrific midday heat; plants would parch and die, birds would be listless, water scarce and foul; and the curse of a low ten-inch rainfall, and drought and eroding wind would play havoc. I had already seen the bleached bones of cattle, camels, and horses; and had seen deserted homesteads to prove the summer battles of man and beast against a ruthless, scorching death.

It was a land of moods and great power. For some hours I sat up on top of Sonder. Birds were busy and tame. One of them was closely allied to the harmonious thrush of the eastern coast of Australia; a type of bush canary hopped through low, flowering bushes. They came close by and finished off the core of an apple. Their life is a constant battle to outwit the wedge-tailed eagles and hawks that make the mountain heights their home.

I went down slowly, trying to save my shoes, stopping along the exposed bridge to peer down into rocky depths to right and left. Far to the west, Mount Zeil, Razorback, and Heughlin, all as high if not higher than Sonder, gradually rose to block the view and circle me in.

Down on the floor of Glen Helen Valley a dingo followed steadily, stopping when I stopped, running a bit to one side in a curve when I shouted, until he picked up a cross-track and disappeared. I camped a mile downstream from Bryan Bowman's homestead. A cloud of dust framed native stockmen approaching behind cattle. They passed the time of day, seemed in some doubt how to judge a man who travelled alone on foot, and rode on, looking back now and then. No doubt they thought I was insane; but I had my own opinion about that.

Across the river a broad series of vertical rock strata stood up some hundreds of feet. Fleecy clouds drifted up behind, and sunset far beyond tinged them to crimson so that the red sandstone slabs rising high up were black and shadowy; and at dusk a very large dingo walked in proud silhouette onto the highest crag and paused awhile, looking down at the sandy river below. He made a magnificent tableau; then disappeared into the silence; and I sat on my swag, still looking at the darkening slabs, and watched large night-birds and bats flutter noiselessly out, one by one.

Daylight dwindled with all its life and colour, but Australia's wild heart beat on into the night. The whole country vibrated and moved with life; mostly silent, mysterious, pulsing, and tremendous beyond the knowledge of man.

CHAPTER VIII
WESTWARD AGAIN

The Mission Board members were to inspect Haast's Bluff Mission, eighty miles a little north of west from Hermannsburg. The morning was spent in loading the big truck with flour, tea, sugar, tinned food, and all manner of stores for sale and free distribution. The Mission policy, strongly backed by the Commonwealth Government, is to overcome the native's tendency to seek the doubtful benefits of town life by providing, firstly, the basic tenets of a living in his own primitive wilderness. It is gradually bringing to the native a sense of comparative values. There are still many whites who defraud the full-blood native and half-caste at every opportunity. The Mission has to act as a protecting barrier between such a parasite and the aboriginal hunting grounds so well placed geographically a hundred and more miles west of Alice Springs, and continuing beyond the South

Australian and Western Australian borders. The native is easy prey to rumour and promise, and drifts easily towards civilization, where sudden contact with white mannerisms quickly undermines any little moral resistance he may have had. It was particularly noticeable during the second world war, when money was cheap and plentiful.

In 1937 a pastoral company was formed, with headquarters at Alice Springs, to exploit much of the country now within the Haast's Bluff Aboriginal Reserve. Had the project been allowed, one of the last native hunting grounds would have been invaded; tribal and family life would have been dispersed immediately without compensation or remedy; a few more wretches would have drifted in to sit idly about homesteads and other settlements, to beg, bargain, and live on greasy scraps of food without thought of diet or balance.

The Mission fought hard against the invasion, and with the help of Dr Charles Duiguid of Adelaide, and others, the threat was averted; and Haast's Bluff Aboriginal Mission, controlled by the Government under the supervision of the Hermannsburg Mission, was the result. The Government has already put down and equipped several sub-artesian bores, and further money is to be spent in providing permanent waters.

We left Hermannsburg at midday, with Pastor Gross driving; and once again I sat on top of a large drum of water behind the cabin of the truck, with Rex Battarbee on another. Pastor Simpfendorfer squatted before us with a shotgun. At every bump the iron roof beneath him boomed noisily. Every few hundred yards a line of kangaroos would start up to right or left, race madly in parallel, and then leap at frantic speed across the road ahead. The good Pastor blazed away in the hope of providing a wayside native camp with fresh kangaroo meat. He announced his progress with disturbing bangs on the cabin roof with the butt of his gun. The usual collection of natives squatted on soft bags of flour, and held on like monkeys over the larger bumps and sandy skids. One was returning from hospital at Alice Springs. Another had attempted to by-pass the Mission on an ill-advised walkabout to Alice Springs: a quiet talk had persuaded him that he would be better off back where he belonged. He seemed quite happy about things, and the lure of 'pitchers' and sly beer was fading before the knowledge of lizards and kangaroo meat ahead. Another native was setting out on a long periodical 'walkabout' into the Aboriginal Reserve, and the truck would ease his feet for a few miles at least.

We turned west from the Finke, crossed over the wire mesh laid on the sandy bed of the Gilbert; and then Gosse's Range stood sharply up before us. The colours of this red crown of solid rock changed rapidly as we curved about it; but basically it was red. Its sides were sheer, creviced, and crumbling slowly. Now, from the west, its colour glowed high into the evening sky. At sunset, Gosse's was dropping starkly down to the northeast behind us, and we were travelling heavily down a long, sandy slope through desert oaks and grass-trees towards the Krichauff Range, which stood up boldly. Before it, a sea of windswept grass was tinted with pink reflection from the red.

Once again the impossible happened. The range

opened up, and we turned south, then east into Kuttaputta Gap. Dusk, and the mystery of driving between rising walls hemmed us in, and made our sturdy motor throb loudly from hill to hill. Several miles along there were loud calls from a massive eastern rock silhouetted against the stars; and Battarbee spoke out of the chilliness of the night.

'Natives camped at Amulda Gap. They'll be in at Areyonga by morning.' We called back to them. Our way down the sixteen miles of valley was heralded by call after call thrown and echoing from one dark bluff to another.

Our nine o'clock arrival at Areyonga Mission brought an excited medley of native men, women, and children. They climbed over the truck, shook hands, peered closely, laughed and got in the way. A few were well spoken. It has been the policy of the missionaries not to encourage pidgin-English. The native has proved himself quite capable of clear diction if encouraged, just as his flair for copying causes him to adopt the broken English flung at him by those who do not know any better. Once a native has grown accustomed to pidgin-English, it remains with him for life and considerably damns his progress.

The day was icy cold and clear, with a slight breeze from the north-east, against which we drove full tilt. Those of us who were perched up high, hung on and shivered. Sonder, Zeil, Razorback, and Heughlin stood up jagged and blue to northward, all not much under five thousand feet; each one defiant, individual, and clear. Each one would alter colour through the day. Battarbee had remained at Areyonga to paint and instruct any natives who showed genuine desire to decorate the white man's paper, instead of red cliff walls.

We passed into good cattle country with grassed flats, and paused beside an abandoned tourist caravan camp, clearly indicated by empty tins and rows of bottles. At sunset Pastor Gross stopped the truck and we all climbed high up on top of the load. Haast's Bluff lay ahead, tilted sideways and standing out clear before several peaks to west of it. The rich blue had the transparency and delicacy of tremendous distance, yet it appeared to be magnified and stereoscopic, and one felt that an outstretched hand might touch it. Deep in the blue shadows, I knew the rock was red, a fantasy of light and colour. Pastor Gross set up his colour camera to record the brilliant crimson and purple of the Mareeni Range ten miles southward, running nearly east and west, and with the soft revealing light of the dying sun full upon it. The Mareeni is nearly one thousand feet high, with a cliff rampart extending many miles like corrugated iron on end. It vanished over the south-western horizon.

Starry night took over, and blanketed Haast's Bluff in black shadow against the stars, while we drove on almost within the silence of its tremendous overhang; and then turned south, then west, to the Mission Depot. On Thursday 12 September 1872 Haast's Bluff was named after Dr Haast, a geologist, of Canterbury, New Zealand, by Ernest Giles, who with his companions – Carmichael, Alexander Robinson, and a little dog, Monkey – stood in awe before the colossal mass, tilting so oddly, and in rebellion against the hills to westward.

Most of the Haast's Bluff natives were away 'bush'.

The little Mission hut of one room was not big enough to hold the party, and most of us slept outside in a night temperature of twenty-four degrees. Old Titus the evangelist was in charge, and had Evangelist Epafras to assist him. These two native men controlled several hundred natives, held devotional services, issued rations with the help of Edwin the storekeeper, ministered to the sick, acted as builders and foremen. They were accredited receivers of kangaroo skins and dingo scalps. Haast's Bluff area is rich in kangaroos, euros, and rock wallabies, and is first-class cattle country for the native stockmen breeding their own small herds. Its choice as a native depot within the reserve has justified itself. Pastor Pech and his wife, a trained nursing sister, have since taken over the spiritual administration of Haast's Bluff, installed a wireless transceiver station, moved the depot to a better position near a permanent bore-supply put down by the Government, and have built a landing field by using a team of native workmen.

The Mission Board members wanted to inspect the cattle country to the west. It was hoped to set up more native stockmen with their own herds of cattle. At 9 a.m., devotion was held beside the ration store. Titus was verger and community leader. I watched the natives come in from every direction; some popped up out of the grass, some from distant bushes. One second there was just bare plain, the next second a string of natives were walking in as though they had been coming for many miles. Mr Weckerts had a large tin of boiled lollies to distribute. No one had said a word. No shout or call was conveyed; but he was the definite goal of many from near and far. They came singly, and in groups, with hand outstretched and a grin from ear to ear; and I listened to the musical 'Xanku', rarely 'Thank you', and now and then '*Owa*'* or '*Culla*'†; but all with the same meaning. Many of them were naked on that frosty morning, particularly the children, who raced all over the sandy flat; and I was not sure whether Titus's call to devotion had called them all in, or whether by some magic they had smelt the lollies miles out across the plains. By the time we were ready to continue westward, perhaps two hundred had wandered in, devotion was finished, and handshaking and mutual admiration once again the order of the day. Haast's Bluff is beyond the end of the Macdonnell Ranges system. West of it a new series begins: strange hills, remnants of isolated eroded peaks, scattered ramparts beginning and ending in disorder, millions of tons of rubble in the valleys. Our journey led first to Mangaraka, a deep-red, isolated old plateau about two or three miles across, standing abruptly on its broad plain, with a gorge cutting darkly in from the north-eastern corner. We parked the old truck half a mile out and walked up a small gully. The red bluffs towered high above us, and ghost gums and cypress pines clung precariously to dizzy ledges. Mangaraka has an important native water reservoir several hundred yards up the gorge. We found its black water deeply shadowed in a swirled-out round hole perhaps eight feet across. It might have been ten or twenty feet deep. A dead rat floated in the gloom. How the natives got down to the water is a mystery. I went

---

* Yes.
† Okay.

with Pastor Gross and Pastor Simpfendorfer on a wild scramble, contouring the base of the main cliff. Our voices boomed and echoed. Nosepeg the native followed with a small attache case. Pastor Gross was out to get all the colour pictures he could. We turned back at an old landslide of fallen boulders, from where we could look out of the gorge and across a broad plain to Haast's Bluff, and to Heughlin, Zeil, Sonder, and Razorback beyond, all a brilliant blue now, sharp and clear in the morning light.

We drove west again from Mangaraka, along the narrow sandy track so seldom used. We were more than two hundred miles dead west of Alice Springs, more than half-way to Western Australia, heading into a land of crumbling mountains aged and shattered beyond all knowledge. Plant-growth lessened, trees were scarce; and immense boulders had rolled from the treacherous heights on either side, out onto the level. It was all disorderly, yet peaceful now after the tremendous landslides that once must have echoed in terrifying force from mountain to mountain. We passed Blanche's Tower, twin-peaked and crumbling, arid and barren, the remains of a great mountain. Beyond Blanche's Tower, Mount Palmer came up squarely, still in defiance of time's edict that all mountains must crumble and die. We passed Palmer and went on, twisting in and out between the fallen rubble; and late in the afternoon turned towards a strangely smooth southern wall of the valley, and walked up to a narrow crevice of red. Water had been rushing from the hills at rare intervals over millions of years. This was Tallaputta, the location of an important spring. The rocks were smooth, and we scrambled over boulders of mauve, grey, and purple, with the red long ago scoured out. Cypress pines and ghost gums found sustenance. No doubt their probing roots had followed cracks to moisture many feet below. Tallaputta Crevice ended at a spring running down a red wall some twenty feet high, in a grotto of ferns and moss and clear running water. Nosepeg rooted out some witchetty grubs from the base of a witchetty acacia, and ate while we hungered willingly.

We drove to the north and stopped before the glory of distant Mount Liebig beyond Ianchi Pass*, with the evening light hitting it in an incredible depth of purple. The pass curved before us as a frame; then several miles beyond that another nameless ridge dipped in a curve of brown and red, to frame the broken, saw-toothed peaks of Liebig lying across at right angles. Sunrays and shadow moved slowly across and gave life and warmth to the incredible colour.

---

* Also known as Berry Pass.

ABOVE: Mangaraka Gorge, of red sandstone,
looking back towards distant Haast's Bluff.

BELOW: The red left-hand bluff of Mangaraka.

Looking down into the Standly Chasm,
Macdonnell Ranges, from a northern ridge.

CHAPTER IX
RETURN TO ALICE SPRINGS

The Reverend F. W. Albrecht lay propped up beside his wife on the floor of the Mission truck. Half a dozen natives sat watching an injured girl of about twelve. She had fallen from a swing, and internal trouble was suspected. She lay on a mattress, with blankets, sheets, and pillow. Someone else was going in for dental attention, and members of the Mission Board had completed their active inspection of Hermannsburg and its outposts.

At Jay Creek I said good-bye to them all, and left the truck. Mr and Mrs Ringwood wanted me to stay the night at least; but I moved off across Jay Creek towards the hills, and turned towards the sunset gleaming on Mount Conway, which stood up prominently as the main peak amongst its rugged group. I did not know then that an old native, almost exhausted and breathless, was telling Mr Ringwood of his great worry at 'poor ol' feller go walkabout wrong way for Alice Spring – me go catchem horse – fetchem back!' But Mr Ringwood managed to persuade the old warrior that I was walking on a planned though roundabout route.

I camped beside a shallow sandy gully, and continued at break of day, up beside a running stream of mineralized water that smelt; up into the vivid red of Standly Chasm, ten feet wide, several hundred feet deep, smooth-walled, with bright shadows and towers of red and pink rock jutting up to the north, framed by the walls of the chasm. I went slowly through, then up into the little Standly Chasm, higher and higher, up and on over smooth worn boulders, through crevice, crack, hole and cavern, and out into the sunlight of a suspended valley running east and west. From the higher crests above that again, some time later, I looked back and down the Standly watercourse and across the parallel ranges to the Missionary Plain a long way south. The chasm had been named in honour of Mrs Standly, a past Alice Springs schoolmistress, who taught white children and many brown children. Originally the lower end of the chasm had been known as Gall's Springs, after Charles Gall, of Owen Springs Station, south-west across the Missionary plain at the base of the Waterhouse Range.

The Macdonnell Ranges about Standly Chasm have kinked out of line into a wrangle of peaks and ravines. I went back through the Standly, and then eastward along the rough base of a red crumbling range. There were terraces, broken cliffs, narrow canyons and caves up to the left, and every few hundred yards a rocky gully emerged to cross the mulga plain before joining a main watercourse down towards Jay Creek Depot. Rough razorbacks of vertical sandstone jutted up sharply. They were piled on edge in long bows up to a furlong in length, rising from nothing up to fifty feet above the surroundings, continuing along the valley like the scaly back fins of a great dragon. An oncoming cold made hard work of the rough going, and the load was well over fifty pounds in weight with cameras and water-bottles. Jay Creek meandered down out of the main ranges several miles ahead. I set a course across rough low ridges to intercept it, and at sundown reached the Jay Creek Fish Hole, a favourite hunting and camping spot, and painting ground of Albert Namatjira. The deep red so common in the ranges had given way to granite walls of light pink, grey, and banded grey and white, about a deep clear pool. There were no birds, and the silence was strange and eerie. A sleepless night with a temperature of 102, and a packet of aspirin did not break the cold; and at daylight I put on double clothing to induce perspiration, and headed away slowly and shakily at first, up through Jay Gorge, and out onto rocky country to northward, and then east along an east and west valley through brittle bushes and dead trees. The cold came out in sweats and grunts. After about ten miles the ranges commenced to break up; and an old track led south-east through a low gap in which there was a small spring. A large euro attempted to escape up a broken cliff, turned again and shot past at full speed, then paused on a ridge silhouetted against the sky and snorted loud defiance. I found out later that the place was known as Spring Gap, the head of the Roe River, which I followed, scrambling across its many bends and over the intervening spinifex ridges, which seemed interminable. The high northern face and peak of Mount Gillen was a good guide, and the walk to it straight but tough and rough, hour after hour. A third pair of heavy brogue shoes in a few days of hard walking were falling to bits. The way led on through a wide valley of vertical bands of stone, horizontal bands, tilted stone, curved stone, and immense piles of slabs without order. I passed by the deep shadows of crumbling mountains about Simpson's Gap, and on into Alice Springs to end a tiring forty-mile walk for the day.

The cold had broken up completely.

It was good to see the Alice again, and enjoy a hot bath and lie flat out on a soft bed and stretch away. Old Gran the cook had to have her 'pitcher' taken, with four pet *Moloch horridus* lizards suspended like a necklace on her ample bosom; and several dear old souls newly arrived from Adelaide wanted to know '*all* about the Macdonnells'; whether they would be able to walk through the ranges. And were the savages *really* wild? And had I a gun? Goodness! Why didn't I carry one? Were the missionaries exploiting the natives? And did Albert Namatjira do his own paintings or were they done for him? Could they get a pet kangaroo somewhere? And, perhaps best of all, almost word for word: 'Where might one purchase aboriginal weapons? My husband is most *vitally* interested in the aboriginal question. He *already* has several boomerangs and spears from the Nullarbor Plain, and is *particularly* anxious to get a big collection before these unfortunate people are allowed to die out. I *do* hope the authorities *really* do something about it all.'

The Adelaide business-man told me of the cornet-player, and how several worried people had entrained him for Adelaide. He had played a departing 'Alice, Where Art Thou?' as the train pulled slowly away from the platform; but the cornet-player had travelled only a few hours before bursting into tears. He left the train fifty miles down the line and persuaded a trolley-man to cycle him back; and Alice Springs had wakened to his wailing trumpet up on Billy Goat Hill just before daylight.

Then two Melbourne business-men with English wives drove into town, and went rabbit-shooting to Simpson's Gap, twelve miles to the west of the town. The women brought in two badly mutilated rabbits at dusk, and went through the dark interior of the hotel, calling: 'Chef! Chef! I say, Chef! Where are you?' A bleary individual stood before them. 'Oo y' lookin' for, the berlanky cook?' He shook his head. 'You don't call the silly ol' beggar "Chef". 'Taint a 'im; it's a 'er; and jus' call 'er "Gran" – see!' Eventually they located Gran, who glared at the rabbits. 'I say – Cook,' one of the ladies said. 'Do you prepare rabbits?' Gran's reply was very slow. 'Hmph! How do you like 'em? Baked, boiled, or just plain bloody like you're givin' 'em to me?'

Alice Springs has a certain amount of modern night life. Some of the cafés keep open until well past midnight. People who set out to travel in from places hundreds of miles out often arrive in the early hours of the morning, cold and hungry in winter, hot and thirsty in summer. The sandwich bar had a temporary girl who stomped about heavily from the hips down and threw her arms round like a body bowler in action. 'What'll yez all 'ave?' she asked, while she chewed rapidly, leant on our table, and crossed her hefty legs.

'Ham and eggs!' We all ordered the same. At the next table a reveller had fallen asleep with his bearded face sideways, resting gently on a plate of steak and eggs.

She went away, returned, took up the same position, and quickly informed us: 'They haint no heggs for none o' yez. Yez'll 'ave to 'ave 'am with somethin' helse. What'll yez 'ave?'

She kept on glaring at us at intervals over the modern counter. She did not like our laughter; and we were annoyed to see the tough-looking guy with his face bogged in two eggs. We got out before he lifted his face from the plate.

I stood before Simpson's Gap, slashing several hundred feet down to sever the high red range to its base. The place was beautiful; and from a bank of sand I saw not so much the grandeur of it all, but empty beer-bottles in shallow water fouled by stock, empty tins, and a gallery of names painted in large white lettering on the smooth red rock. A white ghost gum had been shot at. It was all evidence of vandalism – following upon road access from Alice Springs.

I walked out to Emily Gap, six miles east of the town, crossing the golf-course *en route*, set out on sandy claypans. The aboriginal totemic rock paintings are prominent well inside the gap, and so far no one has mutilated them. They were painted well before the coming of the white man, and look as though they will remain for centuries as an important relic of the native ceremonies for which the gap was once famous. Several hundred feet up on the western side of the gap, large caves, reputedly holding the spirit bodies of the dead, look out to massive red walls less than fifty yards opposite. I climbed up. The rock was smooth and polished by thousands of native feet, and the soft feet of scurrying rock wallabies. It was easy to see these rock wallabies from any high point, as they emerged timidly, one by one, from dark cracks, to sniff and peer for the suspected stranger scrambling about their cliff haunts. The range on both sides of the gap is about a quarter of a mile through at the base, several hundred feet high, with flat plains dotted with mulga and watercourse gums to north and south of it. I went striding and hopping from rock to rock in the spinifex along its crest; it was like moving on top of a giant wall separating two worlds of North and South. To north-west, Alice Springs straddled the Todd River, with roofs and tall trees in mottled white and dark green. A large plane droned up from the south over unlimited space and distant low hills. It landed at the modern landing field, glistening silver against the sun, refuelled in a hurry, rose, circled, and came straight towards me on that narrow wall, which seemed to be marching across a continent. Within a few minutes the plane had vanished towards Darwin, nearly a thousand miles beyond the rim of low, irregular hills to northward.

CHAPTER X
EDDIE CONNELLAN'S
DRAGONFLIES

Eddie Connellan is one of the best-known men in the Northern Territory. Not yet forty years old, he gave up jackarooing, High School teaching and radio work, and in 1938 flew forty thousand miles over the Northern Territory in an amazing and exhaustive aerial survey in an old plane. Then, in 1939, he purchased two Percival Gulls, and at the suggestion of the Hon. John McEwen, Minister for the Interior, he contracted to carry ordinary mail by air from station outpost to outpost, in place of the slow, costly camel, packhorse, or motor-truck method. His first aerial mail-run was from Alice Springs via Mount Doreen and Tanami, both beyond the end of anywhere, then via Victoria River Downs to Wyndham and back to Alice Springs. It was pioneering in every sense of the word. He had to pacify those who thought he was mad, and gradually educate those who treated him with indifference. Landing grounds were crude, and in many cases non-existent. Between scheduled mail flights, Connellan gathered a few enthusiastic supporters and worked to build new airstrips and improve the few existing ones at places hundreds of miles apart, bumping over rough desert tracks with heavy loads of equipment and tools in an old Rolls Royce. It was a colossal task; and some hardened old pioneers bitterly resented the innovation until determination and grit and the full value of aerial service, which began to save lives, time, money, won most of them over.

Jack Kellow was Connellan's first assistant pilot; and Connellan and several of the ground staff worked day and night to keep him up in the air, until war broke out and most of them joined up. The proposition reverted to something close to a one-man show. Few of his original staff returned; only two of his early helpers, Damien Miller and Sam Calder, came back, both with the D.F.C. Eddie Connellan's own war service was not officially in the R.A.A.F., but it was certainly all round it and with it. His rapid organization of aerial mail routes and great knowledge of the Northern Territory was much too important to be lost; and he became an important courier and adviser to and from army camps and commando units, and helped the Americans to survey important landing sites, besides running regular mail services in all directions under tough conditions.

In July 1943 the Postmaster-General's Department increased his annual subsidy to £5800 and asked him to organize a new and comparatively small fortnightly mail-run over the Hermannsburg, Tempe Downs, Angas Downs, Mount Irwin, Kulgera, Erldunda, Henbury circuit, to replace a number of costly ground contracts. This was the aerial run I badly wanted to travel over. By 1946 the subsidy had been increased to £10,000 to help him carry his mail deliveries and friendly service to lonely outposts, over the border into Queensland as far as Camooweal. It increased his fortnightly aerial mail routes to more than seven thousand miles, with at least seventy regular landing stops.

Connellan has gone on increasing his remarkable mail service, striving steadily towards his visionary ideal of linking every settlement within the Northern Territory. His fleet consists of two Dragonflies, a Beechcraft, an old Percival Gull, a Hawk Moth, and a closed Tiger Moth for aerial ambulance work under contract to the Flying Doctor Service, by which he covers the Northern Territory half-way up to Darwin. Perhaps the most amazing feature about his aerial services is that he operates at a considerable financial loss, and finances the loss from income received elsewhere; but Connellan has implicit faith in the future, and is organizing tourist flights and facilities wherever he can. Whatever the future may hold for him, his name will never be forgotten in the Northern Territory.

I walked out to his aerodrome, a mile from the town, and arranged to fly over the Hermannsburg to Mount Irwin mail-run. An opportunity to look down over the rugged land I had walked and scrambled on was too good to miss. A blitz-wagon called for me at sunrise and bundled me off to the large landing field south of the ranges; then the little single-engined Hawk dropped down over the top of the red wall, and I met Sam Calder, D.F.C., and a mechanic named Knight. Up we went and flew west at about seventy-five miles an hour. The plane was obviously old, but I had faith in it and the pilot. At five thousand to seven thousand feet it was possible to see the whole east–west system of parallel Macdonnell Ranges, and the watercourses cutting straight through ridge after ridge. Mountains and valleys were all on the march; from east to west was the order. The Roe River, Jay Creek, the Hugh, the Mueller, the Ellery, all slashed through hundreds of feet of red rock, and headed off southward, always south. We flew north of the Waterhouse Range, and south of a large dam on the Hermannsburg Mission lease, filled with water. Thousands of budgerigars, visible even from the plane's height, swept across the dam, turned and banked, and rose and fell. Then we saw the James Range pierced by the wild canyon of the Finke to south-west; and the red, mysterious Krichauff masses beyond; and the western Macdonnells away to the north-west with jagged peaks towering up. Good old Sonder! A grand old landmark, unmistakable, jutting up bold and blue in the morning light. Sam Calder circled the plane a few hundred feet above the Hermannsburg Mission, then landed two miles to the northeast, threw out the mail to a deserted landing field; and off again, southward above the broad Finke between its deep red canyon walls towering above the white sand winding through the spinifex-topped plateau ranges. Calder signalled and pointed, then banked away west to Palm Valley and the Amphitheatre. The massive sandstone below was gashed with long box canyons. At that time I was far too excited to think of possible engine failure. That thought came later in retrospect. Every second of time was too important to waste, and the floor of the little plane was being littered with film-pack tabs. The plane seemed so much at home that the danger of flying over such a wilderness failed to dawn on me. There were razorbacks and peaks, rock monoliths, curved domes, slits and crevices; and hollowed-out pounds surrounded by red hills on every horizon. We turned south again, once more over parallel ridges; not straight in line like the Macdonnell ridges, but curving over many miles; convex, concave, scalloped, and straight up on edge or tilting over, in an unbelievable maze through which the deeply walled watercourses had somehow carved a way.

We passed above Tempe Downs Station, and did not land. Calder informed me that the landing field was out of order and difficult to maintain. The Palmer River twisted down from the Krichauff ridges like a snake, then struck off dead straight to the south-east. The Tempe buildings were so close beside the deep-green trees lining the bank that, from the air, they seemed part of the dry, sandy river bed.

We continued on with the Krichauff hills dropping away to northward, and desert sandhills in waves beneath us as far as the next line of hills straggling about Angas Downs. There we landed, and met W. H. ('Old Bill') Liddle, sheep pioneer of the desert's edge, and his two half-caste sons. Liddle took up desert and plain country between the Basedow and Wollara Ranges, and brought his sheep across country from Oodnadatta. Dingoes raided them day and night; native shepherds lost some; and many died from eating poison bushes. Wool had to be camel-packed nearly three hundred miles to the Oodnadatta railhead. Liddle gave the sheep up, and soon saw other sheep pioneers east of him give up the impossible fight. He handed the management of the property over to his half-caste sons, and changed to cattle. Up to 1947 Liddle had put down nineteen bore-holes without striking good water. He hopes to continue until he gets it. Angas Downs is a mail centre for a few far-out people who come a long way in. The de Conlays of Mount Conner Station, sixty miles south, send a native boy up with packhorses once a fortnight. It is a journey from the Aneri Soak, round the shoulder of Mount Conner, up beside salt-pans and dry salt lakes, across fenceless, lonely country watered by one doubtful well at Wilbia (Wilbeah) Wells. 'Andrews's place' is south-west from Angas Downs, away in the desert, the farthest out of them all. Andrews's has pioneered a desert track over sandhills and valleys like the high sandy wastes around hundreds of miles of Australia's coastline, for nearly a hundred miles from his home at Curtain Springs, past Wilbia Wells, to the Palmer River.

A cheerful greeting at Angas Downs, and on again into the air, minus a few mail-bags, and plus a list of shopping to be done, and sundry messages in the name of goodwill and friendship. The Connellan aerial mail delivery is not a service merely of cold invoices and payment for all services rendered. It is a friendly, helpful, and almost philanthropic assistance and salute to pioneers.

Sam Calder pointed out Mount Conner, the 'best aerial landmark in the Centre'; flat-topped above its crumbling cliff-sides rising well over one thousand feet above the surrounding desert; red; gleaming in the morning light. Far away beyond it, like the top of a man's bald head, deep blue and hazy, Ayers Rock stood up above the light-red sand; and away to the south were the faint blue peaks of the Musgraves.

At Mount Cavanagh a man said: 'I wouldn't go up in one o' them things for fifty quid.' I replied: 'It's worth fifty pounds of anyone's money,' and was the subject of a long lingering look of pity until we left. We turned back at the aerial mail terminus at Mount Irwin Station, South Australia. There it was windy and cold, blustering up from the south over hundreds of miles of unpopulated gibber desert. At Kulgera Station, back in the Northern Territory, we taxied up to the stone homestead, and swallowed cakes, scones, and tea in a modern kitchen. The little old plane went up again, and I reflected on someone's comment at Alice Springs; 'Ten miles or a blinkin' thousand – it's all the same to Connellan's grasshoppers.' I had got to such a stage of faith in this man and his pilots and machines, that I would have set off readily round the world in our little Hawk.

Long tendrils of cirrus cloud had spread from north to south, and moving rays of fanning light crossed the desert. Down again, and up again. This time it was Erldunda Station, the property of Mr and Mrs S. Staines; then over a hilly wilderness of rocky colour flanking the Finke. Far beneath us a sandy track battled towards Alice Springs – the main overland route from Adelaide. We circled above Henbury Station, set down between its flanking sandhills above a permanent, gleaming water-hole in the Finke. Two native stockmen on lively horses gave and received mail; then, off again across the landing ground, a swirl of wind and up over the rich-green river gums of the river, over the mulgas and desert oaks of the sandhills, and northward over rocky pinnacles, small plateaux, canyons; red, brown, light blue and grey, all spectacular; and each feature with individuality and character. Here was a colourful miniature of all the larger hills and valleys I had seen.

Late afternoon was tipping the Macdonnells with red and mauve, and the emerald green of the spinifex on the southern slopes of Mount Gillen stood out clearly. A few minutes later the flight was over.

I received word that necessitated a quick return to Brisbane. Some of my questions would have to continue unanswered. At least a great work was being done by a faithful band of missionaries, and by a wise Native Affairs Administration, which had combined to arrest the death-rate of aborigines in some areas; and there now was some hope of continued survival and even increase, and hope of the successful transition of the world's most primitive people out of their past of dreaming and ceremony and witchcraft, towards an ultimate state of civilized living acceptable to the white man's Government and creeds. But it seemed as if some of the greatest problems had been faced one, two, and three generations ago; and the early work of the pioneer missionaries who had translated the difficult dialects of the different tribes, thus providing a working foundation for the later missionaries, anthropologists, and medical men, had at last achieved some definite result.

I would be back again, somehow, to find answers to many more questions that had presented themselves; and possibly to locate the man who had crossed the desert in 1923.

CHAPTER XI
ONE YEAR LATER

On Saturday, 26 July 1947, a Qantas plane rose from Archerfield, near Brisbane, at break of day. A ground mist broke up in curling plumes, and we headed into the west with a crimson sunrise over dark sky and ocean behind. Captain Cook's spired Glass House Mountains jutted up forty miles northward. We flew 425 miles straight to Charleville and landed in a cold westerly wind. Heavy rain had fallen over most of the 242 miles between Charleville and Longreach; and surface water in bore-drains, dams, and natural watercourses glinted like flashing mirrors. From Longreach we circled above the Thomson River and its big lagoons, and followed the railway line to Winton. A motor vehicle buzzed about on a bush track like a fussy beetle, and then vanished as suddenly as a rabbit into its burrow. The land had drab pattern and a grey sameness; and there was little colour

ABOVE: Totemic rock paintings at Emily Gap, Alice Springs.

BELOW: Part of Alice Springs township, looking towards
Heavitree Gap from Anzac Hill.

Simpson's Gap, twelve miles by road west of Alice Springs.

until we passed above the tiny settlement of Kynuna. From there, a vast sea of pink Flinders grass went on over the horizon to the north-east.

North-west of Cloncurry bare rocky hills ran in parallel. There were vivid patches of red earth and clay-pan, and the first green patches of spinifex; and watercourses leading off to the north-east. They started as black threads, twisting and turning, joining and thickening into deep-green processions of trees marching off beyond all visibility.

At 4.30 p.m. we dropped down over anthill country, swept above a large green lagoon, and landed at Daly Waters, 1541 miles from Brisbane. The locality was explored by McDouall Stuart, who, with his nine men, passed that way in April 1862, on his sixth and first successful attempt to cross the continent from south to north.

Galahs, magpies, black cockatoos, and mickies screeched continuously. The country was well grassed, flat and sandy, timbered with stunted trees. A few natives had pitched their untidy wurlies two hundred yards west of the Daly Waters Hotel, which had a modern electric name-sign.

The people still talked of warplanes, of Japanese landing scares, and of Yanks who flew by school maps and landed on wrong landing strips; and they talked of Black Jack Walker, a famous Australian pilot; and of a new brewery that would tie up the Australian beer market; and of the tourist possibilities of Mataranka. If only they could get Churchill out to Mataranka, it would boom. Their optimism was healthy, and it is just possible that Winston Churchill has even received an invitation from Daly Waters, Australia! The men I dined with criticized and commented on everything from peanuts round Darwin to half-castes and the lack of doctors; and from the Tasmanian hop industry to a certain Brisbane barmaid whose favours appeared wide and varied. One by one they dwindled into the small stuffy bar, and I dwindled off to sleep like a top.

Jack Humphreys, the publican and local agent for almost everything, showed me McDouall Stuart's exploration tree *en route* to the landing field. Two planes came in within a minute. My A.N.A. plane was bound a further fifteen hundred miles to Adelaide, and would fly back north over the continent tomorrow. If only the spirit of McDouall Stuart could see it! Yesterday's Qantas plane had been serviced overnight at Darwin, and was now off on the long 1541-mile return to Brisbane. The A.N.A. plane hopped nineteen hundred miles right across Australia six times a week.

Above Daly Waters, and for many miles south of it, you look down on a broad ocean of stunted trees; endless and, curiously, blue as the sea shimmering in the distance; tremendous and still, and with a pincushion regularity of design on the red desert sand and clay. From ten thousand feet up it all had the grained texture of coloured mosquito-netting. My nose was pressed hard against the window as we flew down Australia's centre line while most of the passengers from Darwin slept. We flew over Lake Woods with its light-green shore and marshes, and then above folded hills running east and west, and down to Tennant's Creek, where every white iron roof is surrounded oddly by many rain-water tanks. The airport is ultra-modern by contrast with the untidy town. A few minutes and up again.

South of Tennant's Creek, broad bands of brilliant-red desert between green forests stretched over the horizon to east and west as if a mammoth brush had been dipped in blood and drawn clearly across a dull-green canvas.

Just north of Alice Springs there are hazy peaks and bluffs to westward, and a tangle of coloured hills to eastward, with the abrupt walls of the Macdonnells to southward. We landed at Alice Springs at 11.30 a.m. on Sunday, and I got out and looked once again at the big red wall to northward, over which we had just bumped and tossed. It was like shaking hands with an old friend.

Rex Battarbee and the Hermannsburg Mission secretary, Ossie Wallent, were in at Alice Springs with a truck. They had helpful sugggestions to take me straight out to Hermannsburg, but I had planned to walk right through the Macdonnells, and explained that I would be glad of a lift over the twenty-eight miles to Jay Creek. From there I would go on through the ranges alone. At 9 a.m. the truck was already overloaded, when Ossie Wallent received word of two men who wished to go to Hermannsburg to have a look at the natives. One of them was from Adelaide, the other from 'somewhere up north'. Wallent introduced me to the two well-dressed men, Chalmers and Vyner. I looked hard at Chalmers, who was elderly, active, and white-haired. He might have been a bank manager, a scientist, a school-teacher, almost anything professional. A chord of memory went groping back a quarter of a century.

'Did you,' I asked with obvious excitement, 'ever take sheep out across the desert country west of Lake Nash Station – about 1923?'

He straightened in astonishment.

'Why, yes!'

He certainly looked astounded.

'Well, you're one of the reasons I am here,' I explained. 'I was at Lake Nash at the time, with the stock camp on Gordon's Creek, as you and your family and caravan and goats and sheep and goodness knows what else went by. We all thought you were stone mad. Never heard anything more about you. You just vanished into the west past Aghadaghada Waterhole; and we didn't know your name, where you were going, or what for. You left us completely dumbfounded; and I've been wondering for the past twenty-odd years what happened!'

We had a few minutes to spare. Ossie Wallent was loaded ready to go, but he still had to see about a pipe, and a bit of tank iron, and pick up a parcel from a shop and medicine from the hospital, and deliver a message or two and deliver this and that from anywhere, and perform a miracle of favours and service for all and sundry. Chalmers took me round to his modern Alice Springs home for a cup of tea; and briefly, and in simple language, told me his story:

'Our trek took six months. We started from Mungindi on the New South Wales border, and arrived on the Sandover on 5 July 1923. Our homestead is now on the Fraser, a tributary of the Sandover, and 155 miles by road from Alice Springs.

'The station is named after my two sons, Malcolm and Donald – MacDonald Station; and now that they have

106

grown up, this unity and loyalty is as keen as the pioneering battling days.

'The wife Cora, myself and four children, two boys and two girls, Jean, Malcolm Charles, Donald Andrew, and Jessie, made the journey. When we arrived Jean was nine, Malcolm seven, Donald five, and Jessie three years of age.

'We made the journey in a covered-in van with a coop underneath holding five bantams. Besides these fowls, which incidentally were quite at home and laid many eggs while travelling, we brought with us seven horses – four harness and three saddle; two of the horses were good for riding too – that is, the harness horses – and we had three hundred mixed sheep, and thirty-five goats for breeding and milk on the road.

'We got a bit of rain out on the desert. That was lucky, and I don't think we had to travel more than twenty-five miles "dry"; but that was enough. It was several years after our arrival before the line between Oodnadatta and Alice Springs was built. During this interval camels were the chief transport. We used to get them to take our wool away and the loading of supplies back. The loading from Oodnadatta was £22 a ton, and £14 for the wool.

'At this time there was a branch mail service by camel from Alice Springs to Arltunga, an almost deserted gold-field ninety miles away from our station. We sent in by packhorses for the monthly mail and purchased supplies from the store there, which was first started by a Mr Larry Rosenbaum, who ran it in conjunction with his cattle property. It served some of the settlers farther in, as well as gold fossickers and mica gougers.

'Mail-day was a red-letter day, and the return of the packhorses was eagerly looked forward to – a six-day trip, three each way. Natives did most of this work for us, and we have found them loyal and reliable. George – his native name was Coominburra – and a good horseman too, was our mailman for nearly three years. We have always been on excellent terms with the natives and none have been sent to prison by us. Our success with them was due a lot to our being able to talk to them in their own tongue. Personally I can understand a lot of the language, but the rest of the family speak fluently. This knowledge was acquired in a kindergarten way. The game was to name all the plants in the neighbourhood of any place where the boys were working. Donald would have a couple of native boys, and Malcolm would have a similar side. They were all about the same age – all boys together. One side would pick and hide part of a plant, and challenge the opponents to guess its native name. In this way, in a few months, my boys got to know the native names of all the local plants; and not only the names, but the chief characteristics, for they would taste any portion being dealt with and smell it and memorize it.

'This knowledge has been of great service in understanding them, and only recently when trucking a mob of fats, Donald gave his four native assistants their orders in their own tongue.

'You can understand how pleased we were when our first road was made, and connected us up to the main North-South road leading to Alice Springs. It was like someone shaking hands with you. What a difference from no roads at all to a quick fortnightly air service now.

'A bad drought was on when we set out from Mungindi, and to get camps with water and grass for our stock was a big problem; but I found drovers and teamsters most helpful with advice. On one occasion when we were having to go in sixteen-mile stages between water, we were delayed through purchasing a couple of nannies in full milk from a selector adjoining the stock route. We wanted milk for the children. Luckily a car came past, and I hailed the driver, who told me that if I followed a fence running at right angles to the stock route, two miles back, for four miles, I would find a windmill and tank. This was at sundown, and we had to have that water. I took the horses and found the windmill, and got a good drink for them, and brought four gallons back for ourselves. I used the stars as a guide, and the laddies had a big fire burning to bring me in. It had been a very hot day, and a drink for the horses, particularly the two in the van, was essential.

'In 1939 I made over the cattle to the two lads, Malcolm and Donald, with a share for their two sisters.

'Today we own four thousand cattle and six thousand sheep, and breed Arab and Percheron horses. The family are all married and comfortably off, and I have them with their properties adjoining mine. What more could a dad have?'

And that was the simple story of C. V. Chalmers, the man I had wondered about for twenty-four years. Time did not allow him to answer many more questions. Ossie Wallent was back and ready to go, and I had to find out from others how the Chalmers family – parents and young children – had arrived in a land they had never seen before, and wandered with their small stock from water to water, fighting against terrible odds, until eventually the water problem was overcome and they were able to build their own stone house out of the rocks of the earth.

CHAPTER XII
ON FOOT THROUGH
THE MACDONNELLS

I left the Ringwood's home at Jay Creek Aboriginal Depot at mid-afternoon, loaded with shoulder-pack and sleeping-bag, water-bottles, cameras, and films. The day was bitterly cold and raw, and an annoying wind rustled up dust out of the west. A broad easy valley lay ahead beneath a cloudless sky. Large black cockatoos circled and screeched in annoyance at the invader of their wilderness. They kept passing over in platoons towards the setting sun until dusk. The cold blue of Conway* and its surrounding peaks, and the Paisley and Brinkley Bluffs, changed to deep mystic purple, then transformed slowly into liquid gold beneath a strong moon. The cold was penetrating, and the restless

---

* Iloata.

breeze cut through my heavy clothing. I lit a big warming fire of old mulga stumps and grilled a pound of steak, and emptied one precious water-bottle to make a quart pot of strong tea. It was a comforting and fortifying feast, so much that the cold of the night seemed to vanish, and the thirty-five miles of dry going to good water in the Ellery Gap little to bother about.

I walked on in moonlight. Half a mile south a range ran parallel, with its bared rock strata gleaming in the moonlight, and its sides seared with deep shadow. Ten to twelve miles northward a procession of peaks went relentlessly into the west. Startled cattle and horses bolted over stony ground. They were invisible, and their first sudden noise always startling, echoing against the ranges.

At midnight I stopped beside a dead mulga and lit a large fire, with the heavy roots placed to burn some hours; and wriggled into the sleeping-bag. It was a tight fit for a fully-clad man, and uncomfortable; but the drowsy warmth sent me to sleep until nearly daylight, when I woke to a shivering cold and a realization that the fire had dwindled to embers.

That morning I reached the north side of Ellery Gap, forty miles from Jay Creek. The cold wind had dropped and the sun was warming up. Tired feet and limbs demanded at least a few hours' rest at such a perfect camping spot, with clean water, firewood, and soft dry sand to sleep on. The gap had the same din of excited birds that I had heard twelve months before from its opposite end, and there was a boom and echo of distant high wind. Wedge-tailed eagles soared some hundreds of feet above and disappeared

112

beyond the high cliff crests, returning across the narrow strip of blue sky. There were divers, shags, and a pair of comical ducks turning over and over in the water with their feet where their heads should be most of the time. Peewits, kitehawks, falcons, mickies, pigeons, grey butcher-birds, swallows, parrots, and white-shouldered martins passed in and out of the gap in urgent swiftness.

To watch a grand sunset below a sky of mackerel cloud, I clambered up a big landslide of broken sandstone east of the gap. A deep crimson crept over the sky, then quickly clamped intense shadow and temporary darkness before the moon, over the land.

Late that night I heard the restless high wind once again. I had heard it the year before. It appeared to have no direction, and it seemed as if the rocks and hills and trees were gasping in a frantic struggle for life. The calls of the birds in the gap ceased. No cattle moved in to water. This strange, whirling, unseen power of the heart of a continent is beyond understanding; it is awesome, bloodcurdling, yet inspiring.

At daylight the gorge and hills and broad valley were all utterly still and clear like a coloured painting beneath its protecting glass. I walked northward to see the sun rise over distant Conway in the east, and the red glow creeping slowly along the range south of me. It chased the shadows from Ellery Gap. Someone had manoeuvred a vehicle into the valley. Old wheel tracks crossed the clay-pans. A dingo trailed me back towards camp, following along at a safe distance, dodging behind trees and rocks and spinifex, until eventually he got tired of it all, and went diagonally off to the east, looking back every now and then with head raised and paw up ready to dash away.

With fresh water for at least twenty-four hours in water-bottles, and food for several days, I decided to scramble on over the rough southern shoulder of the spectacular mountain about eight miles to westward, marked on one map as Mount Giles, and not even indicated on the others. Visibility was crisp, and the air clear and buoyant beyond normal; but every quarter of an hour or so it was necessary to pause for breath on the long rising bare ridges. Two hours of steady slogging got me to a spinifex plateau some seven or eight hundred feet up the side of the mountain, and far above cattle pads. Razorbacks and red bluffs, pitted with caves, towered high. To eastward, the full length of the grand valley curved right back to Conway about forty miles away. A dry gully started up in the spinifex and zig-zagged for the mystery mountain. I followed it, wondering just how and where it could go through, until a turn disclosed a narrow gap between the mountain and the southern range. Once again close investigation had proved that a distant panorama might hold an illusion. Here was a water-course leading south from a plateau that, from a distance, appeared to drop to the north. The gap in the mountain shoulder was about three hundred feet deep, narrow, rough, and rocky, with smooth tracks of rock wallabies and euros in thousands of years of passing from the plateau to the southern valley now being disclosed. The watercourse was heading the wrong way for my planned route. I turned up a broad rock ledge that ran into a narrow corridor between high vertical walls of the main range, and thus I became imprisoned for the time being with only one choice of route forward. The disintegrating soil and rocks of centuries had crashed into that corridor, and mulga, ironwoods, and cypress pines grew in a matted network that made progress slow and painful, and unbearably hot. It was hours later that I rose above timber-line onto a narrow wall of rock that went zigzagging up the mountain-side like a snake. The total climb was no more than fifteen hundred feet to a point behind the mystery mountain nearly level with its highest crest. The big eastern bluffs were hidden; but the rear of the mountain split up and continued past me in three new and unmapped main ridges, divided by two narrow, parallel, hidden valleys. I was on top of the southern ridge; the other two were running east and west, each a quarter of a mile apart, and containing thousands of tons of broken rocks of all sizes and shapes.

I followed my crest westward. At first, it appeared to continue nearly level and unbroken for some miles, and promised good straight walking through stunted spinifex above all worry; yet within a few minutes I was looking straight down one thousand feet of sheer red sandstone wall into a river bed that had slashed its way through all the ranges. It came in from the north and cut straight through half a mile of walled canyon, then emerged from a dark slit between two hundred and three hundred feet deep, and no more than three feet wide. A large pool of shadowed water, nearly covered by tall leaning river gums, lay at the base of the slit. From that pool, the river continued nearly fifty yards wide, past me, but one thousand feet straight below where I stood in utter amazement. One step forward

115

and the drop would be at least five hundred feet without touching the gleaming red wall; from there on to the bed of the river the cliffs were in terraces, each carrying a few vivid-white ghost gums, dark-green cypress pines, and the shining, green, restless fronds of the *Macdonnellii* cycad palm. My maps had no indication of the place. Rex Battarbee had mentioned the Serpentine at the head of a mysterious and little-known left branch of the Upper Ellery. This must be it. I threw a large stone over and heard the rattle and plomp of several euros, and found one of their many tracks, which I followed cautiously over smoothed bare rocks jutting out above dizzy drops of hundreds of feet. It led over ledge and bluff, beneath overhanging walls, through caves and cracks, and continued by twist and turn. It was nowhere impossible, but a slip might be fatal. The track-pioneering euro of that massive red bluff of crumbling rock had undoubtedly found a way up and down where most experienced men would have searched in vain.

I lunched on biscuits, prunes, raisins and cheese beside the dark pool of mystery and depth. It was impossible to see more than a few yards into the slit, and even a light cough echoed loudly. Miniature pale-blue waterlilies floated at the edge of the pool, and flowering bushes with white bell-flowers grew in the deep shadows beneath the river gums. I went on downstream, through canyon after canyon, and beyond the last gateway of rock there were camel tracks and droppings, and the boot and shoe tracks of white people, obviously made by a rare camel patrol from Hermanns-burg Mission. They evidently had entered the valley at Glen Helen some twenty-five miles or more to the west, and followed the valley over the watershed between the Finke and the Ellery, and then followed the Ellery out through range after range to the broad Missionary Plain, and so back to Hermannsburg.

I headed south-west and then west over low curving hills matted with spinifex. It was a long, hot, dusty walk. In 1927 the late Dr C. T. Madigan of Adelaide journeyed by car up the one hundred miles of valley from Alice Springs to Glen Helen. His car tracks had long since vanished, and only a comparatively disused camel and stock pad remained. His driver should have been decorated and then punished.

CHAPTER XIII
SECOND JOURNEY TO AREYONGA

Hermannsburg was in the throes of a drought. It was early August, with little chance of relief. I came down beside the Finke from the northwest, with a greeting committee of dogs in a long string for fifty yards behind. Old Abel came forward from a shady gum-tree and recognized me. Others followed and stared at this madman who travelled on foot; but there was many a friendly grin of recognition. I was quickly inside with Pastor Albrecht, Rex Battarbee, and Mr F. H. Moy, the new Director of Native Affairs, and his wife. I sat bolt upright, acutely conscious of torn trousers scarcely capable of holding together. Crisis and fatigue were hand in hand.

Mrs Wallent ordered a hot bath in a large iron tub, and said to a native woman carrying hot water: 'You know this man come today?' The reply was preceded by a broad grin.

'*Owa!* I know him that one. Put him patch longa that same one trouser last year.'

Altogether it was a very homely greeting.

General rain had been well below the average eight to ten inches, and storms had been light and patchy; but the missionaries had coaxed large red juicy tomatoes, and lettuce, cauliflowers and cabbage to grow about their homes; and the big native-tended vegetable gardens were holding out under the supervision of Mrs Toysner, with the aid of water gravitated four miles from Kaporilya Springs in the Krichauff Range. Out on the cattle-run, sandy rivers, creeks, and rock-holes were dry, and the customary soaks unreliable. The Mission had sold its sheep, and was faced with the difficult decision to sell or risk keeping the cattle. A good friend of the Mission, Mr Wurst, was boring for water, voluntarily, as a holiday contribution, just north of the rock-walled Mission cemetery, using a boring plant lent by Bryan Bowman of Glen Helen. He had gone down seven hundred feet without success, and had run out of cable. Arthur Latz, the Mission stock overseer, was dejected. If miraculous relief did not come, further stock losses would be heavy. Pastor Albrecht was worried about his native pastoralists. It had been a long, almost hopeless task to set up the several chosen full-blood aborigines with small herds. It was a daring attempt to instil responsibility and sense of ownership and ambition into men whose forefathers had lived in hand-to-mouth fashion. The scheme looked as if it might fail before it got started. Mr McCoy, Deputy Director of Native Affairs at Alice Springs, and Mr F. H. Moy, were both at Hermannsburg to confer on the problems of drought and administration.

119

Pastor Albrecht had promised to organize a special journey, but the Mission camels were scattered, some of them in poor condition, and others with sore backs. He was troubled and anxious to organize something outstanding.

Pastor Sherer came in from Areyonga Depot. We sat on a woodheap and pored over maps. His own camel team was reduced to half its normal strength, and even those were not in good condition. He intended to return to Areyonga with urgent supplies, and hoped to go by the forty-two-mile camel route through the red hills of the Krichauffs. He too was worried by the drought, and wanted to patrol far afield from Areyonga and report on the condition of known waters and springs. I arranged to go with him and wait at Areyonga for whatever might turn up; but once again camels were a problem. We would have to walk and use the camels for essential loading.

Eventually four camels were got together. The first was a hairy, haughty creature. The second was quiet old Paddy, who had to be padded with a light load on a sore back; the third was a nervous, almost blushing young thing, and the fourth, brought in at the last moment, was a noisy, burbling cow camel whose health was causing concern to all, and which we quickly christened 'Lady-in-Waiting'.

Pastor Albrecht instructed Pastor Sherer.

'You've only got a scratch team. Walk as much as you can. Watch out for sore backs, and particularly watch that cow camel in calf. May God be with you.'

We set off, riding at least for the appearance of it, but the pitch and lurch and anatomical discomfort soon reduced me to ground level. Once we had crossed the gravelly Finke and were beyond view of the Mission buildings, Sherer's two native batmen, Mainma and Wanginga, took turns at leading and riding. Natives started up from bush and tree, and walked a chain or so to one side. Somehow, some time, somewhere, they would make closer contact and negotiate for a hand-out. It seemed hard to have to turn them away; but there are always the parasites who find begging the easiest way to exist. Eventually a little girl was juggled up to ride at ease on the front camel with old Wanginga. A tall bearded native with spears and boomerang strutted ahead of his family and waved to us at every opportunity; then pointed to distant landmarks, laughed and giggled, and talked vaguely to the horizon and all in between. His wife followed him. On her back she carried a child of about two. On her head was balanced a large calico bundle with a branch of firewood on top of that. Beneath one arm she held a skinny hunting dog; and two pups trailed behind, whimpering and diving from shadow to shadow. She kept laughing and smiling like a child showing off, and that is a difficult accomplishment when the head and neck are held almost immobile. Eventually the pups refused to travel. The woman turned back and placed a big black foot across the nape of the neck of one pup, gave a quick jerk of her ankle, tossed the pup up and caught it in her hand. She tucked it beneath one arm, and then repeated the performance with the same arm; after which she continued straight ahead into the west after her strutting lord and master – family baggage, youngest child, rations, dog and pups, strewn all about her – a strange, almost brutal picture with the inherited grace of centuries.

121

ABOVE: The curving hills three and four hundred feet high
in the heart of the Krichauff Range.

BELOW: The weird pattern of part of the Krichauff Plateau.

At the southern end of the Serpentine slit through the Macdonnell
Ranges, half a mile long, several hundred feet deep in solid red rock,
and for most of the way only a few feet wide. The left-hand branch
of the Upper Ellery River system passes through the Serpentine.

Wanginga sat the leading camel, apparently oblivious of time; and for some miles I watched him chant softly to the hills, his hands pointing and beckoning in graceful motion to valley and cave in recognition of childhood adventure, or native myth or legend. Lady-in-Waiting commenced to show some signs of distress, and we decided to leave her near a large red sandstone monolith. The shadowing natives stood aside in the spinifex and sand, gesticulating with expressive, begging hands, until they gave up the idea of a wholesale handout and wandered away in search of lizards.

At sunset on the second day the three remaining camels padded slowly and somewhat furtively through the wild and rocky Amulda Gap and moved silently down through the darkness to Areyonga.

The inbred inability of the Australian native to help himself causes him to develop a craving for any available white man's food in the same measure as he loses appetite for his own bush tucker. It is a problem not understood by casual white observers. There are many other features that upset and unbalance him; and if his desires are not understood and he is not helped at this critical stage of his transition, then he is quickly doomed. Many of the primitive wanderers in the vast desert and hill areas west and south-west of Alice Springs were faced with such a condition when, in 1941, large military camps were established all along the overland route from Alice Springs to Darwin, with an abundance of food. The news travelled like magic; the echo of a far-distant war reached out across the desert, and natives commenced to drift in from hundreds of miles out, even from the little-known Petermann Ranges.

Many of them, squatting without food or shelter, were totally ignorant of the white man's wiles, and strangers to their own inherited weaknesses; knowing only that some food might be had for little or no effort.

The authorities became worried over the problem, which, if unchecked, could assume disastrous proportions. At the suggestion of the Hermannsburg missionaries a solution was found by setting up the Areyonga and Haast's Bluff Native Depots, to be built by the Government and supervised by the Hermannsburg Mission. Over seven hundred natives, still mostly in small family groups, were persuaded to turn back towards their own wilderness. Their family life was retained, and they were not disintegrated. It is the future of these seven hundred, and of a few more primitive natives still scattered thinly at far waters out across the great distances, in which the Hermannsburg missionaries have become deeply interested at Areyonga and Haast's Bluff. High-pressure civilization, which has taken white man twenty centuries to build, is too much of a shock for nomadic wanderers who had never known that water would boil.

Thus I was deeply interested, as a rare white visitor to Areyonga, to see what steps the missionaries were taking to cushion the shock of such a recent mass disturbance. My previous visit of one night had left only a fleeting impression of dusky faces, campfires, late arrival, and early-morning departure. We now camped in a small fly-proof concrete hut, simply furnished with table and chairs and wire bunks; and – a refrigerator, presented to the Mission.

Pastor Philip A. Sherer had been in charge of the

Areyonga Mission for several months of his three years of service at Hermannsburg. Prior to that, trained native evangelists had built and maintained buildings, dug wells, distributed stores, collected and paid for hides and skins and wild dog scalps from native hunters, settled arguments, held devotional prayer-meetings daily and a full service each Sunday; distributed medical supplies and given a degree of first aid. A census taken of the year 1947 revealed that Areyonga ministered to 345 natives, including fifty married families, 110 children under thirteen years of age, twenty-four marriageable girls aged from fifteen to eighteen years, approximately thirty old women aged from forty-five to sixty years, and thirty-five old men of similar ages. There were several adopted orphans; and 240 people received Government rations and endowment. There were about twenty-five or thirty young men fit and able to hunt and fend for themselves. There were two families with four children under twelve years, twelve families of three children, twenty-four families of two children, and twelve young families with one child. Men and women were classified old from forty to fifty years onwards, and by disability. The basic rations of flour, tea, sugar and syrup are supplied by the Government to the Mission for distribution by the Mission staff. The Mission gardens contribute important vegetable rations to all aged or disabled people, pregnant women and nursing mothers, and children.

The Areyonga buildings consist of a large general store, two evangelist's huts, three small huts for saddlery, equipment, and a medical dispensary; and the Superintendent's tiny new hut, in which we camped. Plans are in hand for improved quarters, and for a church. Meanwhile, services are held beneath the front or back concrete-floored verandas of the large store, depending on weather conditions. The natives camp and roam at will, here today, gone tomorrow; but often back at the depot on Saturday ration day. In winter days of balmy warmth most of the children run naked, and the men hunt through the hills and deep canyons, naked or with little on. It is a happy, laughing, well-watered land of deep valleys cutting through the thousand-foot-high red plateau of the Krichauffs; but every week or so during winter a bitter wind whips up, usually from the south, and the natives travel with warming mulga or bark firesticks, which they hold in one hand, passing them to and fro in pendulum action before the abdomen.

The white man parks his hat, and sometimes his coat; the Areyonga native parks his hunting spears, and sometimes his firesticks, to glow slowly until wanted again.

CHAPTER XIV
THE SINGING HILLS OF
CENTRAL AUSTRALIA

A rough motor track winds away nearly west from the Areyonga Mission, and out through narrow rocky passes. The valley is locked by red sandstone walls that grasp the downing sun in a crimson aurora at the end of the day. In its rugged isolation in the heart of the Krichauff Range, it has no radio or telephone; but it has music and sound always echoing from wall to wall, and from crag to crag, to continue along a tree-lined watercourse or up into the deep, narrow tributary canyons to the north-east.

All sounds are magnified and held in suspense, and often ventriloquial. The valley is never quiet, and it is at its noisiest with barking dogs and calling natives when the Mission truck battles through sand and rock from Hermannsburg every few weeks with supplies.

I climbed the high red walls of the valley and looked out over vast wildernesses of red canyons, more valleys, and hollowed cliffs, topped by the evergreen plateaux of spinifex and stunted mulga and mallee. Voices drifted up continuously from no particular point, and during devotion and the singing of hymns it was easy to believe that the natives were singing all over the flat sandy floor of Areyonga Valley, which is about a quarter of a mile wide, and a mile long to its first large bend. From there on it runs at least another twenty miles into the east.

The singing was always part of the wilderness. It bounded from rock and cliff, and ran along the watercourse. It was impossible to pin sound to its source. The laughter and shouting, and the lovely singing, and the barking of dogs, the weird blowing of a hollow tube, echoed from rock to rock; and walls and rocks spoke and laughed while moving figures of natives seemed dumb. I watched one afternoon two young men climb a massive red crag until they appeared almost sheer above the Mission. High against the blue sky their tiny black figures stood out. They hurled large stones over the cliffs; and from far up the deep canyon below them their long calls and laughter came drifting back, though they appeared silent actors to a distant accompaniment. It was like watching a shadow-play in the sky.

Morning after morning a clear contralto voice completely dominated the sunrise hour. It defied direction and came from anywhere and everywhere. It was alive, powerful, rich and clear. Its owner would sing part of a hymn, break into loud laughter, whistle, shout, and then sing again with amazing and effortless continuity. The voice belonged to Palatji, the goat shepherd, about fourteen years old; and the echoes belonged to the valley.

I would watch her from a distance while she raced wildly after a bleating goat. She would throw the animal on its side, sit on it, and milk it quickly to the accompaniment of her own amazing voice. The daily routine of Areyonga was simple. Palatji heralded the day; and her loud 'Hey, Billy goater! kiddy, kiddy, kiddy – Hey – ahhh!' woke the whole camp. This would be followed by Lucy, dumpy wife of Wilfred the storekeeper, banging pots and pans over an open mulga fire, while she prepared our simple breakfast of coarse porridge and goat's milk, damper and jam, and rich coffee. Wilfred and Lucy had a little daughter, Audrey, who was generally clean and tidy until mid-morning, and naked and dirty at midday. Devotion followed immediately after breakfast, to which the nearer natives were called by Peter* and Alexander, the native evangelists; then followed medical parade of the sick and lazy, amusing to watch, with Pastor Sherer dispensing medicine and pills and ointments and bandages to all deserving cases. There was no waiting queue of depressed patients; pain was something to joke at. These people had complete faith in the missionaries' power to cure all ills. Alexander was liaison officer and investigator-in-chief. He came in one morning from a long walk. He was old and stiff and tired; but down in Opina Gap some miles away he had found a sick boy who appeared to have no parents or friends. Natives were bringing the lad in. We went out to meet them, and Sherer attended to the

---

* Talbalku.

lad as he lay on an old bag and torn blanket beside Areyonga Creek. General weakness and resultant fever was the main trouble. The lad was a myall, unable to speak a word of English, and apparently had struggled some miles before collapsing; yet he had faith in Sherer, and nearly swallowed the thermometer time and time again. It took many minutes to indicate with pointing and action and expressive grunts that the thermometer was meant to go beneath the tongue and not right down his neck. A prescribed diet of vegetables, fruit, and goat's milk made him much brighter. His hospital bed was beside the creek, his roof the blue sky and stars, and his nurses all who passed that way.

After darkness each evening the full native choir would gather to the command of Peter and Alexander, and squat about small fires at the back of the ration store to practise the hymns that the missionaries had taught them and their ancestors patiently for over seventy years. The natives have fully accepted the white man's worship in song in place of some of their old and barbarous ceremonies. Natives on 'walkabout' have gone out many miles beyond ordinary routes of travel, far out into the Petermann and Musgrave Ranges, and there carried their memory of the hymns and taught the primitive people who had never seen a white person. Missionaries have contacted nomadic myalls who already could sing the words of Christianity, without knowing their meaning.

It was during choir practice that I would leave Sherer for a while, and walk to the middle of the valley to listen, spellbound, to the miracle of rich voices echoing in harmony, and spreading powerfully on and on into the dark unknown like a grand organ.

One Sunday evening the natives came in from near and far. After evening service I talked and gesticulated to them of the coastal jungles of my own country at Binna-Burra, Queensland, and compared tropical jungle trees with the stunted mulgas of Central Australia. The listening group grew slowly until there were some I had not seen before. They were native pastoralists, who had been shepherding their cattle. They had ridden in many miles, and gathered now to form a choir about the low fire. I could face the choir and listen to its full strength, or turn to north, south, east, or west, towards any red bluff or wall, or canyon, and hear the clear, definite returns, one after the other. They sang those they knew best – '*Alkela, alkela, argana nama* (In Heaven, in Heaven is joy)', '*Ta ndolka tjorriramanga* (When I survey the wondrous Cross)', '*Nguang Unkwanga kuterai, Jesua nunala* (Abide, O dearest Jesus, among us with Thy grace)', and '*Altjira rega ekalta kngara tnant jitjika* (Praise to the Lord, the Almighty)'.

The old favourites of civilization are also favourites of these native men and women and their children. 'Silent Night' and 'Nearer, my God, to Thee' are inspiring renditions at any time; but, in the native Pitjentjara and Arunta (Aranda) tongues into which these well-known hymns also have been translated, and with the organ effect of the echoing hills, there is a Sacrament and worship by primitive people in their own wilderness, which is one of the miracle things of this earth.

Sherer and I took shoulder-packs on a morning of bright warm sun and flaring cirrus cloud, and followed the Areyonga Valley eastward in a long and gradual curve between its northern and southern walls, which were deeply gashed with shadowy ravines. To northward, the deeper canyons pierced the main Krichauff plateau for some miles, and were walled in shattered formation and brilliant red, holding all manner of rock overhangs and caves and narrow slits between parting sandstone slabs. In one canyon a perfect red penguin of rock stood up some two hundred feet above a thousand-foot drop. There was no water anywhere in the northern wilderness; the rocks were too shattered to hold it; but to southward the valley's other enclosing wall was of more solid base and foundation, though pierced deeply every few hundred yards by ravines three hundred and four hundred feet deep, with hard smooth beds containing important rock-holes.

The days were going by, and I was becoming anxious, when loud calls echoed up the valley. Natives ran hither and thither. Someone was coming! Narpoo and two other natives in charge of four camels were thus heralded an hour before they appeared in sight beneath a towering bluff. They had messages. Pastor Albrecht had sent native searchers out beyond Haast's Bluff to bring in camels capable of standing the long journey to Ayers Rock. Food for several weeks and Tiger the native guide were following in the Mission truck, and would be 'out' within three days. Pastor Albrecht also would be along personally, to plan the venture.

But a miracle changed the whole picture.

The sky thickened with a white haze, grew leaden and threatening, and natives moved restlessly from one valley to another, pulling down one crude wurley to set up another of spinifex grass and mulga-bushes, only to abandon it within hours and move on again. There were false alarms that the Mission truck had entered Kuttaputta, sixteen miles away, and of wandering natives approaching from the west. Natives were posted many miles out, and amongst them no doubt were the humorists who thought it funny to raise a false alarm; but indecision, restlessness, and a certain amount of irritability were among the nomadic wanderers. Sherer and I sat beside the little campfire well into the night. No stars showed. There was atmospheric pressure within the valley, and the mountains themselves seemed restless.

After midnight, on Friday morning, 15 August, steady rain set in; and by daylight it was raining heavily from the east. Goats huddled miserably on wet crags of rock, and Palatji forgot to sing. Natives shivered within their leaky, makeshift wurlies, and much of the laughter and song died out of the valley; but the rain kept on, swishing and whispering quietly through the hills, bringing with it incredible salvation over the whole land.

It rained steadily for two days and nights, welled up, ran the rocky gullies and ravines, then the major streams, and bogged the country so that camels and horses, donkeys, goats, cattle, and natives floundered deep over clay-pan and grassy plain and valley floor, finding all movement exhausting and difficult. Ultimately everything remained still and waited.

Improved weather with brilliant sunshine brought a general movement of the population. It was moving-day for all and sundry; and those who had not already wandered rooted up their simple belongings and followed

132

the simple instincts of the nomad. A large group of about sixty Pitjentjara men arrived across three hundred miles of rough desert from Ernabella Mission in the Musgrave Ranges. They had come 'up' to contact members of their tribe for initiation ceremonies, and thereby contributed to much of the restlessness. They stayed a few hours, plotting and begging, and then vanished.

I climbed a large hill five miles west of the Mission. Small and large spirals of black smoke curled up out of the valleys and above the hills. The natives had spread far and wide. I met one family heading north-west. The old man tried to talk. I could not understand him and he could not understand me; but he said his musical 'Owa' to everything I said or did, and thus we got nowhere fast except to grin and wave our hands about. His wife circled shyly past, head and body erect, firewood and rolled bundles on top of her dirty matted hair, and the inevitable piccaninny on her back, while she turned every now and then to abuse a crying child some fifty yards behind.

In a fortnight at Areyonga I had learnt much and walked and climbed far and wide into the hills and valleys; but time was limited, and I still had a long way to go. I conferred with Pastor Sherer, and Peter and Alexander the evangelists, and Wilfred the storekeeper. If no word came through from Hermannsburg by midday, Friday, 22 August, I would walk down the rough and lonely camel route beside Illara Creek to Tempe Downs Station, and get a transceiver radio message through to Hermannsburg.

But Friday was a queer day, windy and restless on the heights, leaden sky, heavy, yet cold. Sherer killed a goat, cooked a farewell dinner of roast goat and damper, black tea, tinned turnips and tinned peaches. A group of natives had gathered round the campfire; they were concerned and amused about the man who wanted to walk. Old Alexander's comment was to the point; 'Your name is Ndoinduba – that mean, never stop still; not want to sit about all day. Walk-about here – walkabout there – walkabout everywhere, and not get tight in leg.' At which he indicated his thigh muscles.

It was with considerable feeling that I turned my back on the Areyonga Mission, walked down the bed of the valley, continued a mile through the rocky pass, rounded a bluff and found old Alexander barring the way at the head of about forty natives. Probably half of them were naked, waving firesticks to and fro for warmth. They came slowly, forward. It was a farewell line-up. They shook hands shyly. Then old Alexander stepped forward with his hand held out. 'Good-bye,' he said sincerely. 'You are going a long way. May God go with you.'

CHAPTER XV
ON FOOT THROUGH THE
KRICHAUFF RANGE

Areyonga Creek ran southward across a valley still held within high red walls, which rose to nearly one thousand feet. It has carved its way through gateway after gateway to join the Illara. I went down through them, following the main pad used by goats, camels, horses, cattle, hunting dogs, dingoes, and natives alike, to the wilder country farther south about Bowson's Hole, from where little-known pads radiate off through more hills and valleys.

I looked back now and then to wave to Alexander and his followers, and noticed dark figures on rocky crags; some were silhouetted on the high domed ridge directly above Areyonga; minute, jet-black sticks of movement against a heavy grey sky. The rain had brought emerald-green grass on the narrow flats that had been barren a week before.

Mulga, ironwood, and some corkwood dotted the sward darkly, backed in every direction by the red walls. A large native camp had been deserted hurriedly. The fires still smouldered; some of the wurlies had been built only for a night or two of crude shelter; green twigs and acacia branches were still strongly scented. The winding camel pad went through rocky Opina Gap, then across another flat towards a great cliff running east and west beyond vision, more imposing and a brighter red than any I had seen in the Krichauff Range. The Areyonga disappeared into its gloomy shadow. It was not the ordinary gap through a narrow ridge. This was a canyon through a plateau, known to the natives as 'Lbolba', meaning 'springtime', or 'the time of flowers'. Battarbee had spoken of it as the Beautiful Gap. The walls were sheer and overhanging, but the rocky bed easy to scramble over. The clear pad was marked with many footprints of the Ernabella natives returning southward nearly three hundred miles to their homeland. Scattered ashes had been dropped from their firesticks.

About a mile down in the canyon a lone native approached, naked, walking rapidly, and at first unaware of my intrusion. At about fifty yards he stopped suddenly and leapt behind a large boulder. A loud call brought him out, and eventually he moved quickly and silently past in a wide curve.

After nearly three miles of twisting and turning, the canyon opened onto the grassed plain country about ten miles long and several miles wide, known as Bowson's Hole, the beautiful and fertile Manjura of the natives. The camel pad was now wide and prominent, and soon joined by old disused pads from the west, and the old faint tracks of a large dray impressed deeply into the clay. Towards sunset I passed by MacNamara's hut, well built of sandstone blocks by W. H. Liddle, but now silent and deserted, the tragic monument of an attempt to breed cattle in the wild hill country. MacNamara had worked on a theory that the walled valleys would act as secure paddocks and attract heavier rainfall, besides being blessed with some good natural waterholes, but his theory failed in practice. A few hundred yards out on the plain north of the old house a sandstone cross stands above the lonely grave of P. O'Leary, and wandering natives use the old stone house for shelter.

Illara (Illarara) Creek, now containing the Areyonga, ran wide and clean beside the old buildings, and then turned in a grand sweep beneath tall gums towards, and through, the cliff walls flanking the south of Bowson's Hole. I went on, making good time through further gateways of red stone, and looking for a suitable place to camp.

During the night several horses wandered by and commenced to nibble at the end of my sleeping-bag. Attempts to scare them only sent them beyond the circle of light to shelter temporarily behind a spreading mulga. They took no notice of loud protests, which merely echoed across the creek and back from a cliff. Eventually I found more peace sitting up by the fire.

A daylight start and a couple of hours' steady walking brought me to running water and bulrush pools, continuing until they ran the river for several miles. The place is known as Illara Water, and has its parallel in the better-known and more accessible Parke's Running Waters of the Finke River, forty-five miles to the east. It gives credence to the theory that the vast sandstone masses of the Krichauff Range rest upon an immense underground reservoir, from which the surplus waters emerge at the tilted crest of the reservoir's base on a broad plane, running east and west.

The pools of Illara Water were long and deep, and ducks were plentiful. I climbed a sandstone bluff where the river widened to nearly quarter of a mile between it and the cliffs opposite, some hundreds of feet high, in an impressive formation of vertical slabs separated by deep and narrow cracks. My bluff also was of vertical sandstone. One slip, and I would slither a hundred or more feet into the pitch darkness of one of many cracks several feet wide at the top, but narrowing down to a few inches. It was a thought that brought caution. In one slit the carcass of a bullock or cow had become wedged; and I found two more skeletons in a cave that had been reached by wandering cattle unable to get down again.

It was obvious that the Krichauff and James Ranges were tapering off to the south, with fertile plains some distance beyond, then more scattered hills, and, low down, far away to the right and south-west, the Levi and George Gill Ranges, clear-cut and distant red. Another large sandy watercourse, the Walker, with its lines of large dark-green trees, came down from the west and joined the Illara, to continue as the Palmer, which in turn joins the mighty Finke another hundred miles or so farther on, beyond Henbury Station.

Tempe Downs homestead was hidden in the low hills to the south-east. I plotted a course by landmarks, and

ABOVE: This Areyonga Mission boy seems to have a happy outlook on life.
BELOW: Bewilderment is on the face of many native children new to the mission.

ABOVE: Areyonga Valley, west of Areyonga Mission, Krichauff Range, showing typical parallel curving ranges covered with spinfex and isolated clumps of mulga.

BELOW: Natives at Areyonga Mission. In the background is the echoing Red Wall.

walked on beneath a hot sun. The walking was tough and tiring, over and round sandhills, and through groves of tall desert oaks, across the running stream of the river again, and through untidy mallee scrubs where jumbled sandhills had no order and no pattern. It was a rubbish dump of sand and trees, and the most monotonous bit of country I had ever seen.

A tiny person with pigtails, looking no more than a small schoolgirl, emerged from Tempe Downs homestead, stood in astonishment, then raced away to bring out her mother-in-law, Mrs de Brenni, sen., and W. H. Liddle, the pioneer grazier of Angas Downs. He had driven a ramshackle camel-buggy sixty miles across the desert to southward to return a heavy plough. Explanations and introductions, and invitations to lunch and overnight stay were all simultaneous, while black faces peered round corners of the natural stone building to see the person, who might even be a policeman on patrol, who had walked and carried his own food and water.

Tempe homestead in well laid out, and the main buildings are solidly built in coloured sandstone, which was quarried by a master craftsman and shaped to size out in the hills. Little Mrs de Brenni quickly mounted her pedal radio transceiver, listed as Station OE, contacted Reginald Pitts, the Flying Doctor Service radio officer at Alice Springs – one hundred and fifty miles away by road – and arranged a 'sked'* to enable me to talk over the air with Hermannsburg, Station XH, at 7 o'clock that night. This amazing

---

* A pre-arranged conversation.

little woman, wife of the station manager, Bert de Brenni, who was absent trying to bring a loaded truck through bog from Alice Springs, was running the whole show, cooking, administering and controlling several native stockmen and women, and looking after her two-year-old son.

The sked came through as planned. Mrs de Brenni worked the pedals and manipulated the switches. She was like a doll before a large sewing-machine, pedalling away with the action of a trained bike-rider to generate sufficient current to send the messages out, yet finding breath to say: 'Tempe Downs calling Hermannsburg. Tempe Downs calling Hermannsburg. Can you hear me, Hermannsburg? Can you hear me, Hermannsburg? Over to you. Over to you.' Then she switched a lever and the broadcasting set became a receiver; and back came the voice from Hermannsburg. 'Hullo, Tempe Downs. Hullo, Tempe Downs. This is Albrecht speaking. I can hear you, Tempe Downs. I can hear you quite well. Good evening, Mrs de Brenni. Is Mr Groom there? Is Mr Groom there? I should like to speak to him. Over to you, Tempe Downs. Over to you.'

The miracle of the ages; marvel of space conquered in a wilderness!

Then little Mrs de Brenni again:

'I can hear you, Reverend Albrecht. I can hear you quite well, Reverend Albrecht. Yes, Mr Groom is here. He is listening ready for you to speak. Over to you. Over to you.'

'Albrecht speaking, Mr Groom. I hope you are well. We have been worried about you. As you know, we have had heavy rain – four inches here, more at Haast's Bluff, which has been cut off. Our trucks are bogged; and we have

140

not been able to get supplies out. However, last Tuesday, Tiger left here with another lot of camels and supplies for you, and should be at Areyonga by now. He is a good man. I repeat, he is a good man. He will guide you to King's Creek and Ayers Rock. You can rely on him. He will receive further instructions from Pastor Sherer and follow your tracks to Tempe. You must wait there for him and one other native who will come with Tiger from Areyonga. I received your letter by native messenger from Areyonga. You must not walk across the desert alone. Stick close to your camels. Take them wherever you go, and do not attempt to travel without your water canteens well filled. We have done our best here. You have our good wishes. Trust Tiger. He is a good boy. If you have time to continue south to Ernabella, you may take Tiger and the camels. We are very sorry for the delay....' Then the voice gradually faded, leaving dramatic silence. I was speechless for a moment.

Bert de Brenni arrived before midnight from Alice Springs. He had been bogged many times, and had mail and fresh supplies and promise of an early trip to Alice Springs for his wife and mother. Late into the night the two women talked of nothing else but what they would buy soon. The big truck was unloaded slowly on the Sunday morning by Jimmy the Pig*, a husky native, whose lone grunting efforts were cheered on by his dark mates.

While I was out watching the play of light on the leaning razorbacks of the Arulba Hills to the east, a small cloud of dust drifted up among the tall trees lining the Palmer

---

* Manimani.

River, dark pink in the sunset behind me, and a string of four camels emerged in black silhouette and came slowly in. Six native boys were with Tiger. He handed me a note from Pastor Sherer, whose small handwriting was unreadable in the failing light. Tiger's introduction was wordy.

'I'm Tige,' he commenced, and patted an expanding chest. 'Talkajyerie my name. Mr Albrecht send me – take you Ayers Rock – long way. King's Creek we go, too. Lake Amadeus, too – right up – cross him – I know good place. Last year I take Ol' Man Thommasin an' Misser Borgell from Adelaide, and Metingeri he come, too – lazy beggar, nearly losem everybody.'

We shook hands and immediately his six mates lined up for the same procedure.

'Who are these men?'

For a second there was awkward silence.

'These men all like to come too,' Tiger announced. 'All good boys. I know 'em long time. Good boys. Everybody catch kangaroo – plenty fresh meat – catch pappy-dawg, too. Look about for camella not get lost. Look about for camella not eat poison bush.'

'Only one more boy come,' I said firmly. 'Mr Albrecht tell me that. Mr Sherer write me a note here and say a boy called Tamalji is here with you. Which one Tamalji?'

There was a shuffle in the sand, and I looked into the bearded face of a savage whose eyes gleamed white in the dusk, whose teeth were also white and flashing. At first glimpse he was the wildest-looking man I had ever seem

'This one Tamalji?' I asked Tiger abruptly.

142

The man grunted, muttered rapidly to his mates; and then put his head back and laughed with high-pitched, rollicking, demoniacal guffaws. He could not speak a word of English; but in the dusk he looked powerful, almost frightening, and my acceptance of him only was because Pastor Sherer had chosen him; but I was also facing a common problem in Central Australia. A small camel team had set out with rations in the charge of one trusted native; but others had joined; and so strong is the socialist instinct that they must share with all who came along. I knew that the main rations given in trust would be safe; but I knew, also, that the rations actually distributed and given to Tiger and Tamalji for the journey from Areyonga to Tempe probably had been consumed by the whole group on the first night out.

'Tiger,' I announced firmly, 'you and one boy only can come to Ayers Rock. All other boys must go away now. We start tomorrow morning at ten o'clock.' Then I stumbled through the darkness towards the homestead, hoping the problem would solve itself.

CHAPTER XVI
WESTWARD INTO A
BLOOD-RED WILDERNESS

Tiger was ready beside his four camels, grinning widely. Tamalji, who looked even more savage in the daylight, stood beside him. A few feet behind were three more natives and behind them again another half dozen.

'Ready, Tiger?'

He hesitated.

'These men like to come, too,' he said.

'No!' I snapped. 'Only Tamalji come.'

Tiger was disappointed, though he appeared to be acting a part arranged by others. He looked at a fat youth of about fifteen who stepped forward.

'This one boy belong to me,' he announced. 'Maybe he come?'

I made a rapid mental calculation of what an extra hand might mean to the ration supply and equipment.

'He is a properly good boy,' Tiger continued. 'He only eat little bit tucker. He catchem pappy-dawg, and kangaroo and euro for tuckout and fresh meat for everybody. Good camel boy. Help me a lot.'

I agreed with some misgiving, and roughly ordered the rest of the wanderers away. Tiger soon put the camels up before more relatives waylaid us, and we moved off slowly across the sandy river, heading dead west.

It was my intention to walk at least during the cool of the day, and perhaps ride at midday; but there are few things more monotonous and trying than the first day of a long camel journey. We proceeded half a mile to the first sandhill, then stopped to repair a broken nose-line. Another few hundred yards, and another stop to readjust packs, and so it went on for several miles in a staccato procession of stop and start, only to stop and adjust again. Only one camel had the usual nose-peg inserted in the fleshy part of the nose. The other three were linked in line, eight or ten feet apart, with lengths of thin cord and frayed rope. They were quiet, painfully slow, obstinate, smelly; and snuffled, belched, groaned, dribbled, and spat. The saddles were old; but the large wooden food-boxes and six five-gallon water canteens were substantial and good.

Tiger obviously understood the camels; and avoided their vicious biting and spitting with the agility of an acrobat. His main problem was to nurse them into agreeable marching order, and to get them all moving at the same easy pace at which they will swish-swish quietly on through sand and over clay-pan hour after hour. By midday we had travelled about five miles along a sandy valley and through the rocky Intulkuna-iwara* Gap, to a large clay-pan filled with fresh yellow water. Tiger unloaded the camels, and pointed to numerous recent tracks of natives heading south towards Ernabella Mission. Tiger was becoming voluble and cheerful, though anxious to impress and tell all about his previous trip with 'Misser Borgell and Ol' Man Thommasin'. Tamalji had remarkable energy, and was ready to scout along on foot over sandhills, rocky ridges, or up steep hillsides. Through rocky gorges and valleys his terrific laughter echoed like the devil let loose. Fat little Njunowa watched every movement I made, obviously amused; and gave a running commentary in Pitjentjara dialect to the other two. When he wasn't doing that, he was eating anything he could lay hands on, or dozing drunkenly as he rode.

At the midday halt the three boys threw raw beef straight on the ashes, and Njunowa added a lizard two feet long. I grilled a pound of juicy steak on a green stick, and baked some onions. No chef could have prepared a better feast. Njunowa was amused and watchful, and Tamalji laughed outright until Tiger called them to order, shed his hat, and bowed. There was immediate silence while he repeated grace in the Pitjentjara tongue. It was a simple tribute that I did not forget throughout the journey. The little ceremony was repeated quietly before and after every meal.

The track led into a broad valley separating the red

---

* Carpet Snake.

Levi Range, two miles southward, from an unnamed and lower parallel ridge running across the north. There were acres of golden cassia-bushes in bloom, white daisies up since the rain, and odd parakeelia in bright purple points over the light-pink sandhills. On clay-pans and in shallow gullies there were light-blue bell-shaped flowers on bushes waist-high, and a dainty white heath. Black cockatoos circled above us and flew in wavering formation into the west, just as they had flown over me in the Macdonnells some weeks before. It seems to be an evening habit. Strings of Tempe Downs cattle started up at a distance, ran closer in, circling and sniffing, then with a sudden snort and flurry, and up-flung tails, they would wheel and thunder away half a mile or so, to turn quickly and stand in simulated anger awhile before feeding quietly away. The camels travelled steadily at about two and a half miles an hour. It gave me time to wander off with cameras and water-bottles north or south of the route, up on to the low hills and outcrops, or over the few sandhills that seemed out of place against the red walls of the Levi. Tiger called loud commentaries and advice with much pointing and waving of battered hat.

'Everything going all right. We all right. Tiger knows good track. We go a long way today – allaway. Make camp – thataway,' pointing well ahead up the valley with a small mulga camel-switch. 'You want to ride? Maybe you get tired walkabout all day.'

But I preferred to walk. I had plenty to think about, and plenty to see. By mid-afternoon I had named the four camels. The leader was a small hairy cow camel with sudden temperamental turns. I gave it the name of Cranky Beggar, with variations. The second, a large, lumbering brute, was already known as 'Ol' Man'; and Tiger declared he was very old, very reliable, and that his filthy habits and noises were harmless. The third camel was a timid, dark-eyed cow, quickly christened 'Darkie'; and the fourth, moving along slowly and heavily, at the rear, breaking the leading line every mile or so, was named 'Lady-in-Waiting' (the second). Tiger was worried about her. 'Maybe tonight little camel come up belong to that one. Maybe she go two, three, four days. I dunno; but I think little camel come up sometime all right. No good. We can't travel with baby camel. Must kill him – we go long way today – allaway – thataway!' And another pointing into the west with his mulga switch. 'Come on – Ol' Man! you'm good camel; not cranky feller. You know me – you know Tige. You know – I'm take you an' Misser Borgell and Ol' Man Thommasin, las' year. Come – *on*! You know this road.'

Tiger's definition of a road meant anything from a dingo track to a highway.

We camped about eighteen miles out from Tempe Downs Station, within a great red-walled bay of the Levi* Range. The heavy rains had swept the floor of Petermann Creek clean, and the fresh marks of birds, snakes, kangaroos, and some other creatures I could not recognize, were clear and numerous in the rippled sand. Tiger found fresh water beside a large gum-tree, watered the camels and turned them towards the towering cliffs. They hobbled off, nibbling at the mulga-shoots, and were soon silent in

---

* Ngarkinti.

148

the dusk. I took stock of all our food and utensils. The missionaries had sent out tinned fruits, tinned meats, sauces, jams, honey, syrup, dried fruits, bacon, a large bottle of brandy, and first-aid equipment, many packets of biscuits, potatoes, a bag of onions, beetroot, carrots, kohlrabi, nuts, cheese, oranges, prunes, plenty of tea, and not much sugar; but somewhere along the route, eating utensils had been forgotten. Between the four of us we had two plates, one large Bedourie camp-oven, one iron pot, three mugs, one spoon, and one large knife as the only cutting implement in the whole turn-out. It was with an inward sense of humour that I realized that I had two valuable cameras and many films that filled one whole camel-box; but no clock or watch between us, no compass, pocket-knife, needle, string, mirror, or axe; we had no tent or cover in case of rain! no lantern, torch, or means of artificial light.

In some ways we were a ragtime show; but what of it?

I mixed several dampers on an old piece of bagging – the first for many years. They were particularly good, but the boys were not enthusiastic. Tiger informed me: 'Bread, he much better he not got too many hole. Treacle run away too fast!'

The following day was Tuesday, 26 August. It might have been the beginning of spring. We got away early in the deep shadows of the hills, and twisted away up the valley through further masses of flowering yellow cassia, and within three miles turned south round the shoulder of spectacular Mount Levi*, which faced the west like an

---

* Ngangkali.

immense three-tiered rainbow-cake in colour. I scrambled over its rocky sides and watched the camels half a mile out, several hundred feet below, curving about as they slowly changed direction. South-west, the eastern end of the George Gill* Range, rose up above the broad barren flat separating it by several miles from the Levi. Fantastic cloud-drifts floated over during the whole day from west to east. We lunched beside a long waterhole and sent up some ducks. Tiger had a gun and two cartridges to last him the whole journey. I was unarmed, my most serious weapon being a box of matches. The eastern end of the George Gill Range is strangely spectacular. At a distance it appears tremendous, sheer, and almost overpowering, but close approach across the broad clay-pans kills the illusion. The heights fall back into ordinary red rock slopes, and closeness brings some disappointment. We went slowly between the two ranges, then, with the George Gill now to northward, turned west again along its southern base. The camels were on their best behaviour; but for some miles the scenery was decidedly monotonous except for fantastic cloud-drifts over the hills. Just before sundown we moved out of the mulga on to a natural runway continuing for nearly three miles, about a furlong in width. A plane could have landed almost anywhere along it. Kangaroos were common, and two emus raced frantically across the runway. I dropped some distance behind to study the clouds colouring-up towards sunset, and to watch the camels in silhouette as they moved slowly and silently along the

---

* Aluruka.

strange wide pathway that seemed to head directly into the crimson orb of the sun.

It was hard to imagine anything else but peace in the world.

At sunset, Tiger took a long shot at a kangaroo at about sixty yards' range, and saw it stumble. He leapt from the leading camel, raced after it on foot into the mulga. Half an hour later he walked up beside the camel line, exhausted, and tossed the carcass down on the pebbles. 'Got him – he go close up Oolra*. I been run – and – chase – him – and just about when I close up fall over meself, him fall over first.' One pellet had entered the chest. Tamalji whooped and laughed; picked up a stone, smashed it into sharp flint edges, and disembowelled the animal swiftly. Ol' Man Camel got an extra load of bleeding, furry carcass, thrown over the tucker-boxes. That night we camped in a mulga thicket, with the George Gill Range standing up silently half a mile northward, and to southward the desert stretched on a hundred miles to Oolra and Kuttatuta†. A brilliant moon played havoc with racing, tossing clouds, piled them above the range, threw them aside, and rode merrily above them until midnight, when the clouds darkened and thickened, and it drizzled until morning, with a bitterly cold wind gushing in from all directions.

The camels roared and moaned, grunted and protested, and twisted away from the stinging drizzle, broke leading

---

* Ayers Rock.
† Mount Olga.

lines, and gave trouble until nearly midday. Progress was slow and interrupted. At one stage Tiger gave a loud yell and pointed to a broad expanse of green. Tamalji rolled from his perch on Cranky Beggar, and he and Njunowa went racing wildly over the flats. I was left walking beside Tiger, who was leading the team.

'Pituri,' Tiger explained. 'We take plenty back to Areyonga people. We get three shilling a sugar-bag, sometimes get more.'

We travelled through about a hundred acres of the pituri, growing about three feet high, very much like tobacco. Tamalji and Njunowa darted through it, selected and pulled leaves, and piled them in bundles on the camels until we resembled a travelling market garden. Hardly had that period of excitement passed when two large dingoes leapt away from the rotting carcass of a large calf, and raced for the shelter of the hills. I pointed them out to Tiger. Within a few seconds Tamalji and Njunowa had left the camels once again, and were running after the fleeing dingoes.

'They go catchem pappy-dawg,' Tiger explained. 'Lot of wild dawg in this country. Have little pappy now. Tamalji know 'em track everywhere. He catch 'em. You see. We take pappy skin back to Mission and sell him to Gov'ment.'

About a third along its length, the George Gill plateau-topped range is severed by a broad pass out of which emerge Bagot's Creek and Stokes' Creek. More pituri grew in the piled-up sand beside the fresh-water Walpmara Springs at Bagot's Creek. Three miles farther on we crossed Stokes' Creek, a broad watercourse of sand emerging from its

152

canyon in the red hills, to disappear a few miles south of the range into the sands of the desert.

So far the George Gill Range had been somewhat monotonous and less spectacular repetition of the curving red bluffs and intervening gullies so common to many of the ranges within a hundred miles; but west of Stokes' the escarpments changed rapidly. Oddly grotesque shapes and huge domed outcrops of sandstone stood up above the plateau. Some were like mammoth red animals of a prehistoric age; some were isolated monoliths, hollowed with caves and terraces. It was like looking up to a gallery of leviathan figures modelled from the past. The walking at the base of the range was heavy going in sand, and I had to proceed cautiously to avoid sharp twigs and thorns. The small creek at Kathleen's* Rock Hole emerged from a low wide red canyon. An uncertain wind whipped up from the south-west and annoyed the camels. Tiger halted and unloaded them; I built a fire that scattered smoke and cinders in all directions; and then Tamalji and Njunowa came in silently from converging directions, stood about moodily for some minutes; then, as always, characteristic of them in disappointment, Tiger's consoling remark in English: 'Maybe those pappy-dawgs cranky beggars today. Catch 'em all another day.' A few seconds of continued silence, a reply muttered by Tamalji in guttural Pitjentjara, and the three men burst into violent, continuous laughter, with Tamalji's enormous, high scream drawing a look of haughty concern even from the squatting camels. I had

---

* Ipitilkita.

never seen or heard any man, black or white, laugh with such physical power or volume as Tamalji. His laughter rose up and up, until it seemed to reach a crisis where it could continue no longer; and then down from his amazing high guffaw with a long-drawn, dying scream of finality.

It was enough to wake all the skeletons of the desert.

Sand in the tea, sand in the damper and meat, a belching, stinking camel, paper and clothes blown about, worried the boys only for a few seconds. Each incident was followed by temporary solemnity, giving way to riotous laughter.

Njunowa had brought in a bunch of spinifex. He patiently stripped each needle to get at a rare gum substance no larger than a pin's head, used to fasten spearheads.

Reedy* Creek, some eight miles ahead, was our destination for the night. I left the camels with the three boys, and clambered up on to the terraces above Kathleen's Rock Hole, and turned west-north-west along the crest of a ridge that had the regular formation of a parapet. The camels plodded slowly along half a mile out on the sand, and perhaps seven hundred or eight hundred feet below the crest, waving in and out between mulgas and tall desert oaks. The trees were spaced with mathematical regularity, so that near at hand the straw and pink of the desert sand and grass was the base upon which the deep-green blobs of the trees stood up sharply; but, twenty, thirty, and more miles southward the trees covered the desert in a continuing dark-green mass that went on and on over the flat horizon.

---

* Lilla.

At one point right on the centre horizon, a low faint-blue dome curved a little above the horizon. Was it Ayers Rock? More likely it was some unmapped, little-known mountain beside Lake Amadeus.

I clambered over a prominent red bluff half-way between Kathleen's Rock Hole and Reedy Creek, and found on the plateau above it running water and long rock-holes from the recent rain. White daisies were flowering against the red rock. The camels still moved in parallel; but about a hundred yards south of them two emus moved cautiously in the same direction, obviously unseen by Tiger and his companions.

On the western side of the neck of the large bluff, where it joined the main range, an immense cave continued beneath a jagged cliff for about two hundred yards, and just below it a stream gurgled down a deep ravine. The cave held remains of old native fires and some sandstone slabs about a foot across, originally flat, but now hollowed with the grinding and pounding of native food throughout the years. High up in the walls and shadows were crude rock paintings of lizards, birds, snakes, kangaroos, and circular symbols. It was a monument to the tragedy of dispossession; with yet another probable tragedy of the future if ever this deserted living-place of an ancient people is desecrated by the signwriting of the white vandal.

I scrambled down the gully, and eventually overtook the camels as they were about to turn a rocky corner into Reedy Creek. The bay in the range is about a mile deep and a mile across at the mouth, shaped like a horseshoe; the sandy floor is almost flat, and the cliffs curve about, high, red, and sheer, giving close protection from most of the winds. Surmounting the cliffs, the eroded sandstone domes and monoliths stand up like the buildings of an ancient city. I estimated some of them to be as high as a six-story city building, each one separated from the next by a shadowy crevice in a maze of deep passageways that would take years to explore.

The camels moved slowly in to anchor and looked about with obvious interest. They evidently sensed the end of at least one important stage in a long journey, and moved faster. They knew of water ahead, good feed in the trees, and even a little saltbush a mile or so out. Tiger talked to them, and there seemed to be a bond of understanding between man and animal.

'Come on, you ol' camella. We been make good time, an' you all sit down here an' walkabout all day tomorrow. I take everybody up King's Creek – hey?' A riot of laughter from Tamalji and Njunowa. 'Ol' Man – you know'm this country las' year with Misser Borgell and Ol' Man Thommasin. You tell all these other cammella where good tuckout tonight – get him all fat and full to go 'cross desert. You tell 'em all camella Tiger take you all Lake Amadeus country an' Ayers Rock. Must drink plenty water. Don't you all run away. Everybody go cranky beggar at you!'

More laughter, and Tamalji's high, bloodcurdling scream echoing from the cliffs. We moved up beside the creek with its sheer white, fine sand, running water, tall, graceful, and spreading gums over the sand with no undergrowth; all encircled by the gleaming red cliffs!

We unloaded and camped beside a shattered gum-tree. The tree had been cut and barked deeply with an axe. Its bared weathered timber had clearly marked on it, some ten or twelve inches high, the initial G, by explorer Ernest Giles or W. C. Gosse between October 1872 and July 1873. The tree won't last very much longer. A few more years, and it will fall or burn away in a desert fire.

I rolled out a large damper, sodden, and only half-cooked in the drizzle of the previous night. Tiger came forward. 'You good cook now; that bread good one.' I cut it in two. It was solid dough; but Tiger was enthusiastic. 'Don't throw him away. He is properly good bread; no got little hole everywhere for treacle run out.'

This time I laughed with them; and perhaps it was the peace of the place, or perhaps the associations of years ago when Gosse and Giles moved over Australia's heart in their epic explorations, returning again and again to the cliff-bound haven for water and rest; but I felt a deep contentment and well-being. Within a hundred yards of the camp Reedy Creek descended from the George Gill plateau in a waterfall of its own, delayed awhile in a deep gloomy pool about which there was a small fringe of reeds, and then continued some miles into the desert, to vanish into the great depth of sand like all the other watercourses of the George Gill. The tall, white-boled trees were of vivid green, drooping like willows. In summer, no doubt, it would be a hot inferno of heat radiated from the rock.

A moon sailed up over the eastern walls, and once again tossed light clouds about. Curlews, owls, and frogs called; and a bright patch of moonlight played on the G marked on the decaying tree within ten feet. It was easy to skip back

ABOVE LEFT: A study in black and white at Areyonga Mission.
ABOVE RIGHT: Father and son, Areyonga Mission.
BELOW: Stalking a euro, Areyonga.

River gums near Bowson's Hole, Illara Creek, Krichauff Range.

over the intervening seventy-five years. Ernest Giles had approached from the north-west, and named the range after George Duff Gill, of Melbourne, who had helped to finance his expedition. Apparently he named Reedy Creek, Penny's Creek after Mr Penny of Yorke Peninsula; King's Creek after Fielden King of Gottleib Wells and Black Rock; and, as he continued east, he named Stokes' Creek after Frank Stokes of Coonatto; Bagot's Creek and springs after John Bagot of Peake Station, the Levi Range after Philip Levi of Adelaide, the Petermann Hills and Petermann Creek after Professor Petermann of Gotha, and Middleton Ponds after A. D. Middleton of the Darling River. Giles wandered up and back, eastward, then westward, eastward again along the southern base of the George Gill; but nearly every attempt to penetrate the wilderness of its canyons and ravines was met by hostile demonstrations from many natives.

W. C. Gosse reached the George Gill up from the south in July 1873, turned and went south again. Either man could have carved the big G, now being flecked with moonlight three-quarters of a century later.

It was a strange night. Tiger stood up and sang a hymn, patiently encouraging the other two boys to follow. Heavy clouds overwhelmed the moon, and a slight drizzle set in and continued until an hour before dawn, when all trace of cloud vanished suddenly, and the bitter chill of fine weather penetrated my sleeping-bag. I lay awake, waiting for daylight; but before there was any definite light in the eastern sky, one lone sentinel of a vast feathered colony called somewhere down the creek. It was a clear note I had never heard before, continuous and determined, obviously a signal. It was followed immediately by a bird chorus that filled the whole valley, and continued rapidly for several minutes, as though every bird within the encircling cliffs was determined to greet the day. As daylight strengthened the chorus died down to many scattered chirps.

We breakfasted before sunrise, packed some food, and set out on foot on the three-mile walk to King's Creek and Canyon. Our route lay round the base of the range, which curved to the north-west, and now rose abruptly to nearly one thousand feet. There were bushes of blue bell-flowers, and white bell-flowers, acres of a new type of golden cassia, numerous white sandhill daisies, and a bushy wattle new to me. The boys ran from one desert quandong-tree to another, picking and eating the ripe red fruit; and also found edible figs in narrow clefts of rock. We walked in through acres of stunted bushes to King's* Creek, and paused beside MacNamara's deserted old bush hut, built by W. H. Liddle. Built originally of sandstone, saplings, and clay, it had fallen and crumbled. The creek was running strongly; lined with vivid-white ghost gums, in an intricate pattern of velvet white and deep green. The gums were in the bed of the creek with running water at their roots; they were spread-rooted over massive, fallen red squares and straight-sided shapes of sandstone; they were lined along one rock terrace above another, jutting crazily out of narrow cracks high up the sides of towering cliffs that walled the canyon like a great inverted V nearly a mile long.

We all drank a lot of water from the crystal-clear

---

* Watarka.

159

pools; and as we climbed and scrambled, the whole place absorbed a light-pink reflection from the tremendous, smooth red walls above. Zamia palms were dotted oddly here and there. King's Creek and Canyon had necessitated a long detour from the usual straight desert route from Tempe Downs to Ayers Rock; but I would have travelled ten times the distance to enjoy the grandeur and colour of the place. There is nothing like it in Australia. Its past is steeped in native lore and ceremony. It was and still is one of the main waters and hunting places of Central Australia, and the pilgrimage place of nomadic wanderers who feel its call hundreds of miles away. As we clambered higher and higher with extended vision, we could see distant 'smokes' in almost every direction, mostly out in the great native reserve. Tiger and Tamalji and Njunowa held urgent conferences and pointed excitedly to the smokes. They were trying to work out the direction of travel of those who had fired them. Tiger explained some of them: 'Thata one – might belong to half-caste feller – maybe – go out with one camella to get pappy-dawg scalp. 'Nother one – thataway.' He pointed directly south. 'Maybe Ernabella men go back across desert, and walkabout little while in rocky country, spear kangaroo – euro.' He then indicated a line of smokes extending for several miles. 'Maybe someone come up tonight from Petermann country – long way thataway – camp close by Reedy Creek country – maybe we see 'em.'

Tamalji was excited, and leapt from rock to rock, and scrambled up and along terraces. Njunowa puffed his way slowly, and only went where he had to go. He was getting fatter and lazy, and was a bit of a nuisance. Tiger was proud of his childhood country, and patted himself on the chest time and time again with closed fist. 'This one good country all the time. I live here – runabout – when little boy. Good country altogether. Reedy Creek we call Lilla. Bagotty Spring country we call Wynmurra. All good country. *My* country – go all the way across Lake Amadeus and Oolra and Kuttatuta. I take you and show you. Tomorrow – we go 'cross desert? We take them ol' camella – plenty water canteen – we got good tucker – good! We go three, maybe four, days, thataway – right up by lake country – right up Ayers Rock, we go!'

And as Tiger talked and patted, and filled the other two boys with some measure of excitement, we scrambled up a jagged, narrow razorback, rising higher and higher beneath a red bluff, topped with an unbelievable wilderness of red domes; stopping every now and then to look about over a wonderland that seemed to have no place in Australia's 'dead heart'. The stops were twofold: to absorb the grandeur of it all, and to wait for Njunowa's puffing, sweating carcass to labour slowly higher. For once I had to throw all thought of travel by landmark or direction to one side, and patiently follow old Tiger through passageway and crevice between the giant domes, several miles towards the plateau's edge above Reedy Creek. At one point we laboured up a corridor almost straight for nearly a furlong to emerge on the crest of a dome. It was the last of its group to northward. We were now nearly a mile over the rim of the plateau. The domes continued west, then north-west, to curve in a horseshoe several miles across; but in the intervening space a desert of rolling sandhills, seldom seen by white men, had been lifted some eight hundred or a thousand feet up to form the centre of this strange plateau. What enormous and patient power of wind had swept the sands from the lowlands up over the massive red ramparts of rock, to lie and form and move slowly in waves across the flat, saucer-like depression? Tiger's voice came as though from a distance. He pointed to a thin spiral of smoke some miles ahead. 'Somebody walkabout there. Might be catch rabbit!'

What a country!

The proposed route to Ayers Rock lay down past the eastern end of Lake Amadeus, which was reputed to contain treacherous bog. A straight line from Reedy Creek to Ayers Rock would pass over the lake about one-third of the way from the eastern end of its eighty-mile length. Tiger knew of a direct route across the lake: the route where Giles bogged his horses when proceeding south on Sunday, 20 October 1872, and turned back to King's Creek. Tiger was obviously concerned. The recent rains might have filled the lake and bogged its clay-pan approaches. Giles had named the lake Amadeus after a king of Spain.

But Tiger cheered himself. 'Maybe we be all right,' he called out. 'Tiger knows good road that way. S'pose it too much bog, we go – east – turn around lake country – then see Ayers Rock. I know good road across that desert country. You'm see. We go all right. Right up Ayers Rock – sit down little while – look about every place – then we go to Olga country, too.'

As I baked several dampers and boiled meat and beetroot, to save using limited canteen water in the desert, the three boys chanted about their fire, jumping up now and then in black silhouette against the flames. Tiger called loudly into the darkness, and his voice rolled along the red cliffs. 'We go right up to Ayers Rock, and touch him like that—' He leapt to a tree-trunk and patted it. 'We go through desert country alla way, sandy country, crazy country. Tiger takem you. Show'm you everything. Good country. Only Tiger know 'em properly.' Then he would wave his hands about, followed by echoing round of laughter, with Tamalji always first and last, and loudest. 'Camella! Hey! You camella – out there eatem mulga tuckout! Hey! You hear me? Tiger sing out to you. Don't you run away tonight. You stay close about. We catch you tomorrow morning – quick smart – pack up – quick smart. Boss makem plenty damper make you grunt like ol' man. Breakem your back. Breakem tucker-box. Don't you camella be cranky beggar now, or we'm kick your guts in.'

CHAPTER XVII
PUSSY-CAT AND
PAPPY-DAWG COUNTRY

I rose with the birds' chorus of the next morning just as Tamalji and Njunowa crept off in the dim light for the camels. We got away after sunrise, heavily laden with water canteens and rations, and moved with the majestic slowness peculiar to camels, quietly out of that lovely haven; a mile to the entrance, past the eastern sandstone bluff, and out over the sand. It was like crossing a bar to the open sea. These were the real sandhills, extending for many miles, two hundred to three hundred yards apart, and up to fifty feet high. We had to cross them diagonally, leading the camels to the base of one, ascending at a long angle to obtain grade; slipping, stumbling, shouting, stopping to link broken lines of string and frayed bits of rope; 'changing them up,' to quote Tiger's phrase, which meant trying the camels in a different order of travel in line ahead.

I walked and zigzagged from side to side of the route. There was plenty to see: desert oaks with drooping branches, wildflowers on the sandhills, sturdy flowering bushes usually at the northern base of each sandhill, and the clear new tracks of animals, birds, and reptiles patterned neatly on the sand since the rains had eliminated nearly all but the heaviest and deepest tracks that had stood the test of years. Cattle tracks were common up to ten miles out; after that they were rare. At about ten miles we surmounted a sandhill perhaps eighty feet high. Behind us, but low down, the George Gill and its domes above King's Canyon stood up clearly; and away ahead, a very low, dark ridge, scarcely more than a blue line above the horizon, brought a cry from Tiger: 'That's my point. I know him properly. We catch him tonight. We all going good – camella good – everything good. Tiger knows good road. You'm see.'

Eventually the cattle tracks vanished; odd horse tracks crossed our path; but the tracks of the smaller inhabitants of the desert were becoming increasingly clear, as though etched deliberately in the sand.

'Tiger,' I called, 'little track runabout here. What is it?'

Tiger walked over, looked down at a straight line of tracks.

'Pussy-cat walkabout here.'

'Not properly pussy-cat?'

'*Owa!* Properly pussy-cat – like pussy-cat runabout Alice Springs.'

I was dumbfounded; we were at least fifteen miles out from known waters of the George Gill.

'How long pussy-cat runabout here?' I asked.

'Long – long time.'

'When Mission start?'

'*Owa*, long time before Mission start,' Tiger replied. 'Rabbita – he only come to this country little while. Pappy-dawg – wild dawg – been here alla time. Horse and cattle come before rabbita. Pussy-cat he come long, long time ago – before sheepee an' bullocky an' camella. My people tell me – pussy-cat come that way,' he nodded to the west. 'Long time ago – before white people come, big boat come that way and pussy-cat jump off, run about, find 'nother pussy-cat, and now big mob pussy-cat everywhere, run about desert country alla time; eat little birds – lizard – eat close up everything.'

'What about water?'

'Oh, he walkabout long way in wintertime, then in summertime he look about for nice place in hill country—' Tiger's explanation was rudely interrupted by camel trouble. Ol' Man broke his leading line, then Darkie flopped down in a soft clay-patch, bellowed, groaned, and refused to budge. Tiger spent nearly half an hour adjusting the load.

I could not get the cats out of my mind. Every mile or so, we crossed their tracks. They had been roaming the desert for many years. No doubt hundreds had gone a little ahead of the pioneer settlers; but, surely not since William Dampier?

The clean sand was like a book. A week had passed since the rains, but the light-pink sand was clearly marked by

166

birds, lizards, snakes, large insects, mice, rats, kangaroos, cats, an odd dingo, emus, wild horses up to twenty miles out; and, as we kept heading south over this tremendous ocean of sand, the unmistakable soup-plate marks of wild camels. 'We must look out for wild camella,' Tiger declared seriously. 'They see us first, they come up quick and fight our camella. No good. Make lot of trouble.'

Thus on the crest of each sandhill, I paused awhile to search each trough for any sign of trouble. By midday the four camels had settled down to a steady pace. We stopped awhile, unloaded, and boiled up, glad of the shade of a desert oak. It was to be our longest day of travel with the camels. At about twenty-two miles out we passed three miles west of Tiger's low hill, which he called Alatoota. Somewhere on its uninviting top there was an important rock-hole. The general elevation had risen very gradually some hundreds of feet, and from a high crest I stood awhile in late afternoon amongst flowering heath and looked back over the twenty-odd miles of a saucer depression of sand waves, one after the other, in an ocean of green-topped pink rollers. It was not difficult to imagine movement, so that the whole panorama seemed to move and surge and swell on towards the distant cliffs of the George Gill.

We camped nearly thirty miles out from Reedy Creek, on a bare flat between two large sandhills. There was promise of a chilly night, and clouds had commenced to pile and toss fretfully. Tiger was proving himself a particularly reliable leader. He was proof that a primitive native could be christianized gradually, and imbibe a strong sense of honour and duty. Tamalji was still the wild savage. I guessed that the Christian teaching of the Missions meant little more to him than a routine associated with a source of food. The call of the wild was still uppermost in him, and would dominate his reasoning for years to come. Njunowa was young and irresponsible, and I could see much difficulty ahead of him. Christianity so far meant nothing to him. The primitive living of his forefathers was now a generation or two behind him. He had little awe of tribal ceremony, and many of the ways of the white man were comedy to him.

But we had grown into a team; even if I felt a little annoyed at Njunowa's laziness and voracious appetite, and his off-handed impudence of giggle and underhand comment, Tamalji was in his element in the desert. He wandered, as I wandered, on foot, always somewhere before or behind, or east or west of the line of travel, eating quandongs and berries from small bushes, uprooting and pushing over witchetty-bushes to devour the large white grubs found in the roots, stamping violently about a newly dug lizard's tunnel to block the entrance and imprison the lizard before digging it up quickly and bashing its head against the nearest tree. Then, perhaps, there would be the cry from Tiger perched on the leading camel: 'Pappy-dawg! Go thataway – maybe got li'l pappy somewhere!' And off Tamalji and Njunowa would streak over the sandhills, Njunowa puffing well behind. Excitedly they would go, yet in silence, following the twisting trail of a dingo slut roving in search of food to feed a hidden litter. At such times Tamalji had no sense of duty to the camels. The lure of the hunt and money for the scalps led him on, and I felt he would have little hesitation in deserting me for a litter of pups. It was always during these absences that the camels would play up badly, or a load shift; and I would become annoyed at the absence of the hunters when they were wanted most. The more the incidents occurred, the more reliable old Tiger proved himself. Back the two boys would come, sometimes together, usually separately, with Njunowa puffed and silent. There would be no greeting, merely a sidling up as though nothing had happened, and after a period of monosyllables one of them would make a humorous remark, and Tamalji would start off again with his screaming roar of laughter. But there were the occasions of a kill, when Tamalji would return with four or five or more small dark pups to throw their lifeless bodies beside the skinned pelt of the mother – silent evidence of a battle with a snarling female dingo protecting her young.

The end of each day had its own routine teamwork: a quick unloading and hobbling of the camels, the lighting of two fires, sorting of rations for tea and breakfast – damper, meat, onions, spuds, tea, and sugar for the boys – and then I would sit beside my larger fire and boil a pot of onions and potatoes, and grill a large slice of steak, still fresh and good in the winter coldness; but it was diminishing rapidly, and the lonely tin-opener would soon be in constant use. The boys never ate without grace offered by Tiger, who patiently waited for me to attend.

We had just eaten on the first night out from the George Gill. Tiger had returned grace, and we were standing about the fires, listening to the clink of hobble-chains. Tiger was cheerful, as always.

'You camella, eat you dinner close up tonight.

Don't walkabout every way. You ol' cow camella; don't you have little calfie tonight. We can't keep him. Must knock him on head. I tellem you now, so you b'ave yourself, and listen properly to Tiger! You'm all hear me?'

Chilly night had fallen, but there still remained a continuous chirping, as of many birds.

'Tiger,' I said, 'what's the matter with all those little birds – not gone to bed yet?'

'That one not little bird,' Tiger answered. 'They all lizard – we call 'em Iltjiljara.'

'But where are they?'

'They all sit down under grass and spinifex.' Tiger waved a hand about to indicate the many clumps of spinifex. 'They cheeky beggar; call out for you; tellem you country belong to him, and we must all go away. They like to see moon come up.'

The chirping was all round, as of hundreds of lost chickens. The sunset clouds had broken, and there was a strong low moon in the east. I walked quietly out through the clumps of spinifex. From beneath my feet, under the nearer spinifex, from clear, clean patches of sand, the chirping continued loud and unabated hour after hour, well into the night. It ceased only at the sudden clouding of the moon well after midnight. A spasmodic drizzle set in, and the rest of the night was an uncomfortable, cold, and miserable wait for dawn and hope that the weather disturbance was temporary.

Progress was slow in the fine pelting sleet and drizzle of a grey morning. Visibility was limited to a few hundred yards. The camels broke away, 'went down' to sulk and bellow, and bite savagely at Tiger, who was like a Jack-in-the-box – up and down from camel to ground. Tiger was worried; his landmarks were shrouded beneath low cloud, and his sense of direction was not to be relied upon.

A man's booted footprints crossed our way from west to east, and within twenty feet several camel tracks headed in the same direction, one behind the other in the telltale manner of pack-camels. We evidently were not alone in the vast desert wilderness. Judging by the tracks, someone else was within a short day's journey. Tiger came up. 'That must be track belong to half-caste dingo-scalper,' he announced. 'Maybe that smoke we see from King's Creek country – maybe this man been out in Petermann country – catch pappy-dawg scalp. Maybe go this way and get water in Alatoota country. Rock-hole there; but too many cloud sit down now to see smoke.'

Nevertheless, Tiger lit a large clump of spinifex. The flames leapt and crackled in the volatile grass, churning up and up in dense black smoke, and quickly spread over many acres. They brought an answer some hours later during a lull in the light rain. A single smoke-signal rose from a low point of rock on the south side of the Alatoota Hills, about ten or fifteen miles a little north of east.

Towards evening we scrambled up an isolated outcrop of shelving sandstone. The clouds had dropped low again; but from its crest we looked south over a monotony of sand and trees, continuing on wave after wave. Tiger was worried. He had hoped to sight Ayers Rock and check his direction. To westward, a heavy rain-shower blackened and shadowed the desert, and hit us with a racing swish that

171

sent the camels into a snarling tangle. Within a few minutes it had passed, leaving behind more than half an inch of rain that had vanished into the sand as fast as it had fallen. Since the George Gill I had not seen the slightest sign of a watercourse, gully, or depression in which water might lodge and stay long enough to ease the thirst of any living creature.

We moved slowly on to a mulga thicket at the lowest, hard clay point in a trough between sandhills, barely in time to beat a second downpour. We soon had two large fires blazing away, the camels unloaded, the saddles and equipment stacked in an attempt to divert as much water as possible; and then we stood up without shelter of any sort to face the long night ahead.

It rained heavily until midnight, then drizzled fitfully. The leaping, hissing flames caught the falling rain in scintillating jewels of light. There was a certain grim humour in the situation; and out in that desert of reputed scorching barrenness I would have paid well for an umbrella. There was no wind, and the swish-swish of rain through the trees, and on the ground fast softening into bog, was a sound I grew to hate. The journey ahead would be difficult. It would be necessary to avoid, as far as possible, the boggy depressions between the sandhills. The heat of the fire sent the dampness of my clothes drifting up in steam. I was worried about Lake Amadeus. It lay only a few miles ahead; but the rain probably had filled it or bogged its approaches.

The three boys crouched about their small fire for several hours, chanted and talked; then they coiled up in wet blankets and slept until daylight about a dead fire. They rose in subdued misery, moved over to stand silently about my fire. Tiger could have sold out for sixpence. Tamalji's laughter was a memory; and Njunowa shivered violently even while he almost grilled his naked body over the coals.

A temporary break in the weather came at about nine o'clock, during which the boys slowly brought in the camels, loaded them silently, and began the difficult task of travelling south through a land that had now absorbed at least four inches of rain. The troughs were difficult and treacherous and unavoidable, the sandhills tough and strenuous at any time. Tiger took the leading camel and proceeded cautiously, winding in and out, sometimes almost circling completely about to avoid the soft patches. The extent to which the earth's surface had softened was incredible, although all trace of water had vanished. Within an hour the heaviest rainstorm of all blackened the west, raced up, and pelted down with hissing fury. The camels became frantic, bunched up, groaned and bellowed, and refused to budge until the rain had passed towards the east, and the first bright sunlight for two days turned the desert into a gleaming mirror for just those few fleeting minutes until all sign of water had vanished again. Tiger mounted the leading camel. 'Come on there! Rain all gone!' Tamalji's screaming laugh rose up and down the scale, and even Njunowa called up enough energy to trot away in search of witchetty grubs. The camels got into line and strode out at a good three miles an hour, through patches of soft ground, over the sandhills, and across the valleys, for there was a new zip in the air that could not be denied. A high sandhill barred our way, visible across our path a mile or more to the south-west, and continuing on unbroken to the north-east. I watched the camels mount it slowly, diagonally, with Tiger turning in the bright sunlight to call to the labouring animals behind him. He reached the crest, took off his hat and waved it wildly:

'There lake country – close up now. No more rain! We soon catch him now.'

CHAPTER XVIII
AMADEUS – LAKE OF MYSTERY

Perhaps two or three miles ahead, visible between the trunks of the dark, scattered, desert oaks, the vivid white of water and gleaming beach extended many miles right and left. Perhaps ten or fifteen miles to the west Ernest Giles had sighted Mount Olga, in October 1872, and so impressed had he been by its distant horizon of domes that it led him on towards the lake, where for several days he floundered about in an unsuccessful attempt at crossing. The name of Olga was attributed later to the elusive goal at the suggestion of Baron von Mueller.

Thus, with the spectacular lifting of the cloud masses, higher and higher, Tiger and I ascended a high sandhill in an attempt to sight Mount Olga and Ayers Rock beyond the waters of the lake; but in that direction the clouds were still dark and bunched. To the north-west, and nearly behind,

ABOVE: Thousands of red, wind-worn, sandstone domes line
a great U about twenty miles in extent at the western crest
of the George Gill Range, Central Australia.
BELOW: Turning into Reedy Creek, George Gill Range.

ABOVE: The lower red ramparts east of King's Canyon,
with mulga-bushes and domed clumps of spinifex.

BELOW: The glowing bright-pink and red cliffs of King's Canyon,
at the western end of the George Gill Range. The bed of the valley
is filled with a tropical tangle of white ghost gums, palms, and
ferns and flowering bushes around running pools of water.

an unmapped hill rose abruptly. It was clear blue against a distant angry black cloud. A patch of roving sunlight topped it in sharp relief. The waters of the lake spread away before us, running into many fingers and bays. Tiger shook his head. 'Last year I bring Ol' Man Thommasin and Misser Borgell across lake – and it properly dry – we cross him easy, thataway—' he pointed to the sheet of western water. 'Now, too much water everywhere. This time, we must go long way round – long way, thataway—' He pointed away to the south-east where the lake broke up into long placid fingers, framed within mile after mile of clean sandy beach topped by bushes and low trees. The clouds were piling up again in magnificent grandeur over the loneliness of Australia's most mysterious lake; more often parched and dry, radiating the sun's terrific heat of summer, treacherous with salt-pans and bog to wandering animals. I was enjoying a sight of it seldom seen by man.

'Tiger,' I asked, 'which way Ayers Rock?' He was searching in the south-west.

'Can't see him. Too many big cloud; but must be thataway all right.' And he indicated the south-west with a quick drop of his outstretched hand. 'We must go right up to lake now; then we must go round saltbush country for long time. Maybe tomorrow we see Ayers Rock.'

We moved in to the northern shore of the lake. The desert and its tall, majestic desert oaks, and the frail desert grasses and clumps of spinifex, continued right to the beach, and then ceased abruptly where hardened rock-salt formed a dividing layer between the bed of the lake and the plant-life of the desert. There were many camel tracks along the beach and in the shallows. Although the water was undrinkable they probably fed and existed largely on the juicy saltbush lining the beaches. The sheet of water continued unbroken over the western horizon; but it probably was nowhere more than two or three feet deep, and much of it only a few inches deep. I walked across the crackling salt encrustation, and gingerly to the edge of the water. There was no perceptible movement of wind or wave. The water had a green transparency for some yards out; and from there on it was like a vast sheet of mercury reflecting every cloud in the sky. Two or three days of hot weather would reduce the size of the lake by hundreds of acres.

The camels refused to travel close to the water's edge. We continued slowly through the afternoon, running each salt-pan finger a mile or more to its end, crossing the brown, muddy saltbush flat at its tip, twisting, turning, unloading and reloading as the camels jibbed, stumbled in the mud, and went down. Tiger persuaded and cajoled; Tamalji laughed and shrieked and did little more; Njunowa conveniently disappeared; but by evening we were round the worst of the fingers, and at the base of a great bare, pink sandhill, rippled with wind, where Tiger informed me would be 'properly good camping-place', because 'no more bad lake country now. Tomorrow we all go thataway. *Must* see Ayers Rock soon now. Two more days, and we go *right* up – close. Puttem hand on him properly.'

We made camp at the base of the sandhill; and within a few feet an arm of salt water went out to meet the lake, directly into the west, taking with it the deep-crimson reflection of the sunset; still, silent, incredibly dead, yet beautiful.

I sat on my swag and ate boiled onions and stewed prunes, and a tin of bully-beef. Perhaps thirty feet away, the three boys squatted beside their fire and tore at the remains of the kangaroo, now stinking and dirty. In thanksgiving, they had said Christian grace in their native tongue, and preferred the kangaroo to the tinned meat I had offered them. My last impression of the passing of that day was the sight of the four camels a little to the south-west, dark and shadowy, one after another in silhouette against the dying crimson, moving off in search of trees and bushes they liked.

About midnight the sky clouded over again, and blotted out the millions of brilliant stars that had ruled for a couple of short hours. A sharp shower hissed viciously over the sand before dawn. I could hear it half a mile away. It brought me from my sleeping-bag in time to rebuild the fire. The heavy rain killed the sunrise and heralded another dirty, grey day. In absolute disgust we sat and ate in silence. The boys were thoroughly subdued once again. I was frankly worried. If the bad weather continued another day or so, I would have to abandon the journey and turn eastward. The sky looked hopeless, and particularly bad to westward over the course of the lake. Apparently the vapour rising from the long sheet of water was causing much of the trouble. It made me wonder to what extent an inland sea might influence the climate of Central Australia. I climbed the high sandhill. It was perhaps eighty feet high, pink, almost bare, and several hundred yards long, ending at its western end as a sloping tongue into the lake. The only plants about it, like a fringe of hair round a balding man's head, were low, flowering wattles, and bushes of white heath. A sharp breeze whipped up from the south, the clouds jarred, tufted, and broke with the rapidity of minutes; and then far to the south-west, but very low down, I could see the unmistakable flattened dome of Ayers Rock, Oolra of the natives, pale mauve against the troubled sky beyond, pale mauve above the dark green of desert trees and the dull pink of the sandhills. I shouted to the boys and pointed. They jumped to their feet and called back, and Tamalji's great guffaw set them off; and, within another minute, fat little Njunowa was streaking to eastward for the camels.

CHAPTER XIX
AYERS ROCK ON OUR SKYLINE

We crossed a boggy clay-pan and called good bye loudly, almost profanely to the lake behind us. Ayers Rock lay ahead, and we had actually seen it. For several miles the smaller, jumbled sand-dunes and broken troughs and court-yards, now crowded with stunted mallee, prevented further glimpse of our goal. Then we emerged onto a parkland of spinifex dotted with desert oaks only. There was no imme-diate sandhill high enough to obtain a view. Another arm of Lake Amadeus, completely unknown to Tiger, forced us a further delaying three miles to the east; but the way round it was comparatively easy. Away in the west the dull ceiling clouds of the morning receded, and then banked up again in the high, cumulus, atomic-bomb manner of sudden local storms. There was great contrast of vivid-white cloud and jet black beneath, dark curtain of rain and clear sky to right and left; sunlight and shadow side by side, falling rain and gleaming light. Towards midday the piling-up took on organized movement, and the storms passed before and behind us, one after the other, with a flurry and rumble of thunder, to continue on over the eastern horizon. The extraordinary procession went on for some hours, until one raced up and loomed high above us. It was impossible to avoid it. There was a blackening-out of light into the mystery of dusk, a heavy wind, a revolt of the camels, and then the heaviest rain I have ever known ripped leaves from the mulgas and pelted us like hail. The camels broke their lines and became frantic. Tiger muttered in annoyance; there was little he could do. Tamalji crouched beneath one of the large tucker-boxes, moving as the camel moved; and fat young Njunowa raced naked behind a mulga and laughed hysterically until the rain ceased as suddenly as it had started, and brilliant sunlight, gleaming on the wet surface of the desert, followed it.

The water soon vanished, and we continued our journey as though little had happened, with Tiger leading the camels cautiously round the sodden patches. There followed a strange game of hide-and-seek. The sandhills had once again taken up definite formation, and as we led the camels slowly over them the wide panorama of desert sands and bared crests and the intervening troughs of mulga clumps broadened and became higher, with Ayers Rock always ahead, forty miles away; and now a mile or so nearer, gleaming in dull pink.

Our approach was slow. Now we stood on a crest of windswept sand and saw its distant, breathtaking oneness and stillness; now we dropped between the sandhills, and our world closed about us in a desolation of sand and spinifex and scattered mulga. It was a goal coming slowly nearer, changing colour slowly in the afternoon sun; until I saw away to the right the pale, ethereal blue of many domes splitting the horizon like the temples of an ancient city.

'Kuttatuta!' Tiger spoke excitedly.

Mount Olga! The elusive goal of Ernest Giles, and still seen only by few men. It is the most awesome sight I have ever seen. It has light and colour far beyond the imagination of those who will never see it. Even without Ayers Rock and Mount Olga on the one skyline, the winter sunlight slanting across the sandhills has its own powerful beauty; but the picture, disappearing and reappearing tantalizingly before me at the summit of each sandhill, had the silence and grandeur of ages, and the power and simplicity of space and wilderness.

That night we camped right on the crest of a sandhill, and I sat and watched the colours slowly fade until Ayers Rock and the temples of Mount Olga darkened slowly into the night.

It was a gusty, cold night, with damp sand beneath us, and a longing for morning.

We travelled well all the following day in brilliant sunlight. The Rock loomed nearer only with an almost annoying slowness. Shortly after midday I defined a large area of eroded terraces and caves on the northern cliffs, some hundreds of feet high and as broad, resembling an exposed human brain. As we crossed crest after crest the brain grew into sculptured relief, scarcely credible as the work of time and wind, but seemingly the result of mechanical drills and chisels.

The boys sent up smoke-signals; but no answers came back from the Rock. Its solitude was real, and there were times when I felt I was approaching the immense coloured tomb of a dead age into which I had no right to look. The solitude might have been even more impressive had it not been for the continuous bell-call of a bird, which surely had beaten place and distance with its high run of notes and contralto base, ventriloquial, distant yet all about, and invisible. Tiger informed me: 'That one Bunbunbililila!' and at my attempts at repetition Tamalji threw back his head and laughed aloud.

The camel has been called the ship of the desert. As I walked, abstractedly, a hundred yards or a quarter of a mile to right or left of the four of them, I seemed to be viewing a moving story from a distance. The vast immobility of sandhills and intervening troughs was so much like an ocean stricken into stillness that the camels were like tiny boats moving ever so slowly over waves without life. Every now and then I would turn across the heavy sand, weaving in and out of the prickly spinifex, and move in closer to the camels, and for a time, once again become part of that slow-moving fleet, moving so slowly that Ayers Rock and Mount Olga seemed still years away as a reward only to be gained at the end of life's span.

There were times when I reflected upon the unusual journey in search of respite and clarity of thought. The world and its problems were distant and unreal. The great monoliths in the desert were so symbolic of defiance amid desolation that I could not fail to gain at least some strength of purpose at sight of them. I do not think any of the few white men who have travelled slowly towards them in a desert pilgrimage, have not been affected in the same way.

Each sandhill challenged effort; it was tough, slow going, heavy walking while loaded with cameras and water-bottles; but practice and strategy helped so much that I realized there is a definite art in crossing a sandhill, an art in crossing the troughs between, and healthy practice for the senses in plotting direction without fail. Down in the troughs all signs of Ayers Rock and Mount Olga disappeared, and I had to note angles at which the sandhills ran, and then pick a lone bush or bump on the next sandhill as a landmark, approach steadily until the sandhill loomed high up, then a steady, leaning ascent up the soft, bright-pink sand with feet evenly spaced to avoid slipping; up and up, a pause for breath with the corrugated crest still against a brilliant sky of cirrus cloud; up again, and – once again Ayers Rock still dead ahead; no mistake, no lost ground. Direction checked and found correct!

A quick check to sight the camels; for that was important. Now they were up on the crest also, perhaps to the east, moving slowly over, now they were out of sight down in the next trough. Sometimes I would draw ahead of them, perhaps a mile, looking back every few hundred yards to check again; until, reaching the crest of a chosen sandhill higher than all those for some miles round, I would squat in the cool sand and enjoy the warming sun of Central Australia's winter; and study every detail of the grand monoliths still many miles away, but approaching slowly through time and space so that with each sandhill ascent I could note some minor difference of feature, or colour, or shape.

The strange hide-and-seek went on, until when the Rock appeared no more than six or seven miles away, its mass loomed above the sandhills and was never out of sight. The camels ceased their yawing to right and left and increased their pace to an obvious goal. Once again, at sunset, I stood apart from the camp, and watched the setting sun colour Ayers Rock in a fiery red. The crevices and hollows, caverns and overhangs, and blackened line of watercourses stood out in dark shadow and mystery against the blaze of light over everything else; then I raced across the near sandhill, and saw the sun go down in a fan of crimson behind the dark silhouette of Mount Olga.

That night was clear and cold. A heavy dew came down and penetrated my sleeping-bag, and soaked into everything lying about. Before sunrise, Tiger pointed out to several small birds deliberately catching the dew on the leaves of a low mallee-bush. Here then was perhaps one answer to the riddle of where creatures of the waterless desert obtain fluid. The eastern sun painted the Rock once again, this time a light revealing pink. We got away within the hour; our slow approach now accompanied by budgerigars, crows, finches, mulga and ringneck parrots; and a rapid increase of wildflowers on the areas where wandering natives had burnt the spinifex a year or so before, and enriched the sand with ash. One particular bush, about five to six feet high, had golden and green flowers waving up and down in the light wind, remarkably like green parrots in flight. I thought the bush was a type of banksia. Later investigation revealed that it was a type of desert grevillia. Tamalji and Njunowa left the camels and ran from flower to flower, bending low at each bush, sucking nectar from the flowers, and passing on. This was one of the desert delicacies; and I became conscious of much twittering and chattering overhead, and discovered hundreds of grey martins circling above, diving down in our wake to peck at the honey-laden flowers; and always in the distance, the elusive, tinkling Bunbunbililila.

My guess of six or seven miles from the night's camp to Ayers Rock proved incorrect. It took four hours of steady travel to penetrate the encircling belt of mulga sloping down from the surrounding sandhills towards the base of the Rock, which stands in a vast saucer depression, so gradual in its slope from the sandhills that it is scarcely noticeable. The last half-hour of travel was the most misleading, for a guess of a quarter of a mile to the base was made when we still had more than a mile to go. We continued straight towards the towering light-red walls, until boggy ground from the great gallonage of water that heavy rain had cascaded off the Rock, terrified the camels, and I walked ankle-deep in mud, slipping, stumbling, bogging, dodging pot-holes and larger clay-pans, to approach the Rock, conscious of a growing clamour of birds high up on its tremendous walls.

CHAPTER XX
AN ANT AT THE DOOR
OF A CATHEDRAL

The rock itself was now much too big to be seen as a unit. It towered above in a dizzy height of sheer red wall to meet the white of floating mackerel cloud, evenly spaced across a blue sky. High up, perhaps a thousand feet, hawks, crows, and eagles moved and screeched in and out of caves and crevices. The lower walls were painted white with their refuse.

I came to a rock pool, approaching it over fallen slabs of sandstone, and drank icy-cold, clear water, and stood back to watch the long thin stream trickling down hundreds of feet. These trickles occurred every hundred yards or so, and actually, during heavy rain, would create a large number of temporary waterfalls, up to seven hundred or eight hundred feet high.

Tiger was having trouble with the camels. Tamalji was abusing them in his own expressive language. Njunowa was standing aside like a helpless humpty-dumpty, giving forth his hysterical laughter. I went out to them, and found it necessary to deviate round bog after bog, until we eventually camped on a hardened island of ground a quarter of a mile west of the Rock itself.

From the west the vertical strata of the Rock is obvious. It is an immense tilted monolith of sandstone bedding, rising to eleven hundred feet sheer above the surrounding plain, and undermined at its base, in places, by long cylindrical caves, in some cases more than a hundred feet deep. The Rock is reputed to be one and three-quarters of a mile long from west-north-west to east-south-east, and seven-eighths of a mile wide. From a distance the colour of the Rock is never the same, altering every hour of the day; but close at hand it is a light brick-red, with a stucco effect over its whole surface, caused no doubt by the cracking away of small flakes during the terrific summer heat.

With any sort of luck, Ayers Rock would have been discovered by Ernest Giles in October 1872, when he first saw Mount Olga (twenty miles west of Ayers Rock). It was not until Saturday, 19 July 1873, that another explorer, W. C. Gosse, approached Ayers Rock from the north, travelling down a little west of Tiger's chosen route. He saw the Rock and named it after Sir Henry Ayers. Water was scarce, and found only on the southern side. W. C. Gosse and an Afghan named Kamran, ascended Ayers Rock on Sunday, 20 July 1873 – the first time it had been ascended by a white man; and in their survey of the surrounding country, named a point, Mount Woodroffe, in the Musgraves, to the south-west, after the Surveyor-General of South Australia. Ernest Giles was not able to visit Ayers Rock until Tuesday, 9 June 1874, when he followed Gosse's dray tracks in over the sandhills from Mount Olga.

W. H. Liddle, of Angas Downs, had told me to expect an expedition by four-wheel-drive trucks from the Geelong College; but there was no sign of any recent visitors; and Tiger declared that no one had visited the Rock since his own visit fourteen months before.

We set out to circle the Rock on foot. The boys were high-spirited. Tamalji went tearing across the boggy flats, leaping and whooping, and creating running echoes along the red walls; then he disappeared into the mulga to north-ward on the track of a pappy-dawg. It was Njunowa's first visit to the Rock, and he followed Tiger at first in wide-eyed excitement, until I asked him to scramble high up to pose against the main wall. He agreed the first time, protested the second time, and was too tired the third time, after which I gave him up as a photographic model. We stood before the great Old Woman's Cave, over three hundred yards long, a hundred feet high, and undermining the Rock on its northern face. Known as Itjaritjaringura to the natives, it has for countless centuries been a legendary 'dreaming-place' of a woman who sprang from an ancestral burrowing animal of the mole family, no larger than a mouse, to be found in the surrounding sandhills.

I felt like an ant at the door of a cathedral, until Tiger scrambled ahead of me over sandstone boulders, and we entered the great cave. Tiger located old rock paintings, and campfires that had blackened the cavernous roof. Curtains of thin sandstone hung down. I reached up and tapped one with a small stone. It rang out like rich china.

Tamalji walked in from the surrounding mulga and joined us at the eastern end of the Rock. He had missed his pappy-dawg, and was quite disgruntled until he found a bush of native figs; and the three boys rapidly consumed a great number while I wandered on to negotiate a natural moat. The southern walls of the Rock sweep in and out in deep bays or indentations up to two hundred yards deep; and down into each bay a stream trickles strongly from invisible rock-holes. Immense boulders had fallen and piled high. The boys wormed in and out in search of elusive pappy-dawgs, but found nothing. They were more interested in the possibility of financial reward for scalps than in the grandeur of the place.

Various writers have described Ayers Rock as difficult of ascent, when in reality it is a trained mountaineer's job on the east-south-east corner, a rough and steep scramble up at least two places on its southern side, and nothing else but a strenuous and spectacular uphill walk on its western side. On the northern side, the sheer cliffs and hollowed base prevent any reasonable attempt at ascent.

We tackled the easy western route, called Tjinteritjin-teringura* by the natives. It is a bare rock ridge, not much steeper than a staircase, rising from a broad beginning to a narrowing ridge of sandstone, surfaced with the rough stucco pink common to the whole Rock. Tamalji soon gave

_____
* Willy Wagtail.

his wild whoop and screaming laugh, and ran barefooted all over the place. His balance was amazing. Tiger grunted and groaned. 'Me getting old in legs,' he gasped; but he was determined. In desperation he turned to me. 'You feel all right? You not feel like properly old man?' But I was feeling splendid, and raced after Tamalji, who had taken the steep climb in his teeth. Tamalji was defying all known laws of extreme exertion by gulping several mouthfuls of ice-cold water from each round rock-hole. The man had the energy of a demon, and still found breath to laugh in wild abandon.

Njunowa gasped his way up the Rock for perhaps a hundred yards, then flopped on the Rock and rolled out flat on his back and lay spread-eagled for our return. Mount Olga's many domes rose above the sea of sandhills; but there were other mountains beyond, a strange, encircling concourse of rocky silhouettes and distant shapes of the far Petermanns to westward, and the Musgrave Ranges in a chain of peak after peak to southward. Some of them had never been trodden by white men. Two days' travel to westward was the lonely grave of prospector Henry Lasseter, who died of dysentery and starvation on 30 January 1931; buried crudely by friendly natives of the Petermann Ranges, reburied by old Bob Buck, Central Australian wanderer, who now lives at Doctor's Stones in the eastern end of the James Range, south-west of Alice Springs.

There was no trace of Lake Amadeus to the north. It was hidden in its salty hollow only six hundred feet above sea level. The summit, crest, sides, ridges, ravines, shelves, and terraces of Ayers Rock are pitted with hundreds of the rounded rock-holes, capable of holding from a few to several thousand gallons of crystal-clear water from any light passing shower. The recent four inches of rain had filled every hole, until each pool overflowed to the next in a scintillating chain of flashing light.

Tamalji beat me to the top by a furlong. His time for the ascent was about thirty-five minutes. Tiger was still a dot turning the shoulder a quarter of a mile down. A small pile of broken sandstone has been placed on the summit, and the usual summit tin and bottle of names are there. I took out the pieces of parched and frayed paper. I have been on many a mountain summit, and seen many a cairn of stones and bottle filled with names; but none excited me more than those accounts of the past few who have travelled hundreds and in some instances, thousands of miles, to ascend Ayers Rock. In this lonely land it seemed to give the names written in ink and pencil definite reality and personal presence. Goodness knows where they all are now; but here are the names:

7/3/1931. W. McKinnon.

19/2/1932. W. McKinnon.

July, 1933. W. Fuller.

28/5/1936. H. N. Foy, Mrs Foy, Tom McFadden, Stan Tolhurst, Gus Schaller, Bill Morgan, Sydney Walker, Bob Buck, Denis Haycroft, Rupert Kathner, Kurt Johannsen, S. Mulladad.

Nov. 1939. V. Dumas, F. Clune, E. Bails.

7/8/1940. C. P. Mountford, J. E. Sheard.

14/8/1940. C. P. Mountford, J. E. Sheard.

30/6/1946. Lou A. Borgelt, Cliff Thompson, Tiger, Metingerie.

192

Tiger arrived and flopped straight into a pool to cool off. 'My legs get properly tight!' he grumbled, and thumped his cramped thighs. 'Tamalji run about *too* much like big euro!'

Ayers Rock stands through the ages, seldom visited; and most of those who see it now, fly out from Alice Springs in one of Eddie Connellan's small planes. A speck drifting in from the north-east, a droning above the desert sandhills, a roaring, echoing circling once or twice of the Rock – for there is no proper landing ground – and off again, leaving behind startled rock wallabies, and emus racing from the mad noise in the sky. Most of the natives have deserted its cliffs and caves, and 'moved in' to Ernabella and Hermannsburg Missions. Many of them are up at the Areyonga outpost, and turn south on the long walkabout to Oolra, less and less while civilization teaches them the ways of the white man. There is talk of a tourist road to the Rock, and more talk of a proper landing field and a hotel for visitors. At present the Rock is protected from the average visitor by virtue of its position within the Aboriginal Reserve, and no white person is allowed there without written authority and sufficient reason for it to be granted. The Rock is in a similar position to many of Central Australia's wonder spots. Some day it *may* be discovered again by someone with power to unlock the gates of close protection about it now; and unless its protection is made permanent before access is considered, the day will surely come when people will paint their names on its pink walls, steal the native pounding-stones and relics about it; shoot its many birds and unusual animals, and root up the unique plants at its base.

Tiger was worried about camel poison bushes, apparently a duboisia, which grow on the plain south of the Rock. We shepherded the camels to north-west, and watched them closely. My original plan was to leave them and walk with shoulder-packs to Mount Olga's domes, somewhat more than twenty miles to westward. But Tiger was emphatic: the camels must go with us. Njunowa was more than relieved. The idea of a long walk to Olga and back did not attract him at all, and he did not relish the thought of a lonely wait at Ayers Rock.

That night Tamalji unearthed the remnants of the stinking kangaroo killed more than a week before, and cooked it once again on the coals. He was again the savage, naked, chanting, eating as his forefathers had eaten, chewing his pituri wad when it wasn't parked above his ear like a grocer's pencil. I kept to windward, and handed out tinned fruit, raisins, prunes, tomato sauce, and the last of the oranges to augment the feast; but all these things were put aside until the smelly kangaroo was reduced to a few bare bones. Eventually, Njunowa rolled flat on his back and lay curved up like a poisoned pup. Tamalji went over to the corned-meat bag, fingered the remnants of the salted meat from Tempe.

'Stink!' he remarked, grimaced, and spat viciously. His English was improving; but from then on it would have to be tinned meat, goanna, or witchetty grubs.

A late moon came up and outlined the dark silhouette of the Rock, and when it had risen sufficiently to cast a halo at the high crest, I walked quietly away from the camp, turned north out of the shadow, and continued between

ABOVE: The passing of a desert storm south of Lake Amadeus.

BELOW: Lake Amadeus, the mystery lake of Central Australia, after rain.
It is approximately ninety miles long and from two to ten miles wide.
The water, which is salt, is seldom more than a few inches deep..

ABOVE: '...the storms passed before and behind us, one after the other...'
BELOW: Njunowa and Tiger pose before rock paintings
at the southern base of Ayers Rock.

the patches of bog. The colour had dissolved completely, but the shape, height, depth, and shadows of cave and cliff were even more impressive; and there was the suppressed bickering of quarrelsome birds roosting high up in the terraces of the Brain. Unseen animals plopped and moved away in the grass. I moved quietly towards the Old Woman's Cave, but its uncanny depth and a soft moaning of wind drove me quickly back into the moonlight. It was a weird, uncanny walk, but since I had started it I decided to go right round the five miles of the base. It meant ploughing once again through bog and long grass in the extended shadows of the southern side and south-western corner. The most impressive features of the night walk and stumble through bog were the skyline silhouettes of the Rock itself against a few brilliant white flecks of cloud; and particularly so, when back near the camp, I moved in towards the western wall to look at the slit of indirect light between the main sloping wall and a long slab of sandstone, separated by about two feet of space, and sloping upwards for at least three hundred feet. It is a great column, parted from the main mountain, known as the Kangaroo's Tail.

I stood there for some time and saw a black, fluttering shape against a small drift of cloud. It was not a bat; but probably a night-bird off in silent search of prey.

CHAPTER XXI
THE FIRST WONDER
OF AUSTRALIA

Of all the Central Australian monoliths and tors, peaks, and distant ranges the Mount Olga collection of domes is the most misleading. It is mapped twenty-two miles west of Ayers Rock; and from the base of Ayers its domes are clear above the sandhills, light blue in the morning, dark purple against the red of sunset at evening.

We set out for it at sunrise, and I walked as usual away to one side of the camels. Some miles out I crossed the unmistakable imprint of wheel tracks, years old. Someone had evidently attempted the journey by motortruck. Goodness knows when it will be repeated. The sandhill country between Ayers Rock and Olga is not as impressive as that to northward about Lake Amadeus. The easternmost domes of Olga rise no more than five hundred or six hundred feet, and in reality hide much of the grandeur from the traveller approaching from the east. The old camel pad skirted a mile southward, and just before midday I stood alone on a small plain about two miles from the first battery of domes, to admire something more promising in the shape of a great red elephant rising to nearly a thousand feet. The body, head, and trunk were quite clear. It was perhaps half a mile long.

The camels caught up, and Tiger informed me: 'Camping-place long way round yet.' We plunged into rough, scratchy mulga, and continued by a winding route over country covered with loose stones the size of cricket-balls, which upset the camels' placid equilibrium. This was followed by soft soil and some bog as we moved in closer. Tiger added: 'We not camp in Wulpa* (Walpa, Walpina) Chasm. We go up close this way – more quick to look about before dark. We leave camel at good camp and walk right round.' I agreed, and we worked up a narrow rocky gully close beneath a vast wall of conglomerate that once had been a deep red, but was now covered with a mottled grey and green coating of old moss, streaked with the black seep-ages of storm-water from the heights. The smallest dome could have crowned the world's greatest cathedral, and the greatest was a red immensity of rock that would have completely dwarfed the same edifice. They were composed of millions of tons of pudding conglomerate, just as though a giant power had hurled rounded balls of stone, from a few inches to several feet in diameter, into a softer mass; and

---

* Wind.

there they had remained, although many thousands had broken away and were lying about the supporting slopes and gullies. There were fallen masses, larger than city buildings, rounded by slow erosion, but containing a make-up of thousands of smaller, component, rounded parts. The conglomerate did not appear to have the solid strength and oneness of the Ayers Rock sandstone, nor was the general approach from the surrounding plains and sandhills as spectacular.

We unloaded and hobbled the camels, boiled the billy, and had a quick lunch of damper and tinned beef; and then Tiger led the way with all the importance of a trained guide. I followed him up a conglomerate gully, through acres of tiny pink-and-white lilies, up a stony ridge covered with daisies, and into a wide saddle about two hundred feet above the camp. Tiger stood aside dramatically.

'There – now you see – this one *my* country, properly,' he said proudly. 'When I been little boy, I runabout here, long time. My father, my mother walkabout here. This one properly Kuttatuta.'

Not one great bluff of domed rock rose out of the hidden valley now exposed – at least six giant, parallel monoliths of dull red, with the slope of a seventh partly hidden some miles to northward, rose between a thousand and fourteen hundred feet. They were exactly in line, facing the east, and obviously hidden greatly to a distant observer by a further battery of domes, lower and rounder, a mile or so to eastward. On a minute scale, one could model the main battery of Olga bluffs by putting six long, round-topped, red loaves of bread on a table, side by side, separated by a quarter of an inch of space, and increasing the dimensions to fourteen hundred feet high, one mile long, three hundred yards thick, and from fifty feet to fifty yards between each loaf.

Tamalji gave one of his loud screams, and while his echoes ricochetted down the valley before us, from bluff to bluff, hawks and eagles winged and screeched from the heights straight above. We scrambled down into the hidden valley and found a stream still running strongly from the rains; and within a further couple of hundred yards were opposite the great chasm dividing the first and second monolith. The second chasm, between the second and third domes, was deeper and larger, with a narrow slit of daylight through its coloured shadowy length of a mile, no more than a hundred feet wide for most of the way, and fully a thousand feet deep. There was a continuous boom and rumble, softening now and then to a murmur. I felt as though the domes were moving in agony.

'This one Wulpa (Walpa, Walpina) Chasm,' Tiger announced. 'He go right through – long, long way through. Water everywhere up there. Water summertime – properly spring. Rough place in there. Wind never stop. That's why we call him Wulpa.'

We stood awhile before what was surely the organic heart of Australia, with tremendous life and power. Surely all the winds and moods and storms of the continent find birth in the Olga chasms, to move out north, east, south, and west. Tamalji yelled loudly up into Wulpa, and I was glad to move on. The combination of moaning wind far off, and Tamalji's blood-curdling yell, was more than eerie.

The third chasm bent to the right a quarter of a mile in. Its course was clearly defined by beams of slanting sunlight; but much of it remained in deep-purple shadow. Towards the crest of each monolith, where the cliffs curved over, each dome carried a horizontal gallery of depressions or large niches in the wall, evenly spaced, as windows in a castle. One could easily imagine the faces of an imprisoned people looking down the sheer walls.

From each chasm a stream of clear, icy water emerged beneath fallen debris and flowering bushes, to join the main stream running away to northward. I tried to figure the amount of run-off from the great domes even during a minor rainstorm. The total would be millions of gallons, which had to seep out gradually through the rubble at the base of each dome.

Half an hour before sunset we had completely encircled the main Olgas, and were on the western side, looking up into the western end of Wulpa Chasm. The lowering sun penetrated the chasm, lighting its length and depth with startling realism. There was little if any moss on the western side, and the walls were stark red and bare, except for a tiny bush or two perched precariously high on the curving shoulders. It is doubtful if more than one or two of the main Olga domes are scalable. The sides are straight, and the ends too steep to place much faith in the treacherous conglomerate.

That night I listened to the wind howling through Wulpa. It was not pleasant at all. It was just an irritating moan, rising and falling, continuing through the night, chopping and changing. The wind punched its way down our gully to batter us; then it would calm awhile, and return from another angle to blow ashes and sparks all over the camping gear. Sleep was impossible. I sat up half the night and saw the moon rise over Ayers Rock and light up the Olgas gradually. The noise of the wind rose to greet it; and the Olga chasms howled as though in violent protest at our trespass. It would take very little imagination to fall victim to hysterical fear; but the three boys slept soundly enough, curled up each in one blanket with small fires between them, and a low windbreak of mulga branches round them.

Next morning Tiger assured me the wind never ceased.

I told Tiger to pack and move back towards Ayers Rock. I would go alone through the bluffs to get photographs, and would follow the camels later. Thus, a little after sunrise, I moved once again up the slope of flowering lilies and followed a ridge to eastward, far enough to look into all the Olga chasms at once. It was an unforgettable sight, transcending by far the grandeur of Ayers Rock, or anything else I have witnessed in my lifetime. The dome on which I stood was warm and peaceful in calm sunlight, and the distant howling of Wulpa Chasm was like a faraway, dim accompaniment to the impressive stillness of the hidden valley in between and below me. Two or three miles out beyond the circumference of the complete Olga group a heavy ground fog spread out above the sandhills and plains like a snowfield. It commenced to tuft and break up as I dropped down into a narrow crevice, tightly packed with undergrowth for about two hundred yards. An hour or more later I emerged on the slope of another valley to meet three dingoes almost face to face. They paused a fraction of a second, wheeled and raced away while I scrambled hurriedly onto a rough conglomerate outcrop to see more of them. My foot dislodged a large boulder, which rumbled and rolled in considerable noise. The dingoes had disappeared completely, but the echoes started up several euros. They went hopping off in different directions, rattling over stones and spinifex, pausing awhile to look about at this man-made disturbance; a snort, and on again, up and up with incredible strength and grace.

Eventually I scrambled two or three miles east of the main Olgas, and entered a canyon about five hundred feet deep, and less than a hundred feet wide between sheer red walls; and continued up it for half a mile to scramble out on to a rocky balcony that I recognized as one of the front legs of the Elephant dome I had seen the day before. The 'head' of the elephant was now one sheer wall rising a good four hundred feet to my right. The 'leg' was hollowed below me with caverns and overhangs. Rock wallabies hopped and lay round in the sun, unconscious of my presence above them. Movement was impossible without noise, and when I continued downhill they whisked into shelter.

I took a line on Ayers Rock clearly visible against the distant peaks of the eastern Musgrave Ranges, and set a course slightly southward of it to bring me across the camel tracks. Two hours later I moved up beside Tiger on the leading camel, half-asleep in the morning sun. He woke up with a start.

'Which way you go this time? You want to ride camella?'

But the camels were too slow, and I was feeling fit

202

and eager. I tossed up part of my pack on top of the big tucker-boxes, and walked on ahead towards Ayers Rock. Rains and floods had delayed the beginning of my long journey. Now I wanted to get back to civilization as soon as possible.

CHAPTER XXII
SMOKE ON THE HORIZON

Had time been more plentiful I would have turned south with the camels to the Musgrave Ranges, and then followed that range system to the Presbyterian Ernabella Mission at the eastern end of the ranges, within sight of the five-thousand-foot peak of Mount Woodroffe. I had considered the possibility of a long walk over eighty miles of intervening desert to Ernabella. This suggestion had caused some concern to the Reverend F. W. Albrecht of Hermannsburg; and he had communicated by radio, while I waited at Areyonga, with the Reverend A. C. Wright, Superintendent of Ernabella, and discussed fully the obvious dangers of such a hare-brained proposition.

I learnt some months later that Mr Wright had sent two native men to meet me at Ayers Rock, and guide me through if necessary; but they returned to Ernabella a week later without reaching their destination, and complained that there was too much water and bog in the desert!

Ernabella Mission commenced operations in 1937. Its first Superintendent was the Reverend H. L. Taylor. It has an average resident native population of about one hundred and fifty, with several hundred more calling in for brief periods between walkabouts and intermittent employment on grazing properties many miles farther in, towards the Adelaide to Alice Springs railway line. Some of the natives are the most primitive in the land and have had little contact with the white man. They roam a hundred or more miles west through the Musgrave, Mann, and Peter-mann Ranges. Once a year some of them move up on the long three-hundred-mile walkabout to Hermannsburg or Areyonga for man-making initiation ceremonies. The usual route north is from Ernabella to Mount Conner, thence up beside scattered salt lakes to Angas Downs, and through the Krichauff hills to Areyonga. Before the arrival of the white settler, movement was free and easy, and good hunting all the way; but now the natives find their waters fouled and shared by wandering stock, equipped and closed with man-made pumps and tanks; and the hunting is not good. The wanderer is not to be blamed if be relies now on what he can beg, earn, or borrow, so that he often reaches his destina-tion a half-starving, cringing remnant of a once virile race.

The Ernabella staff consists of the Reverend A. C. Wright (the Superintendent), and Mrs Wright, Sister Turner, Miss B. Bills (school-teacher), Mr John Bennett (stock overseer), and Mr M. Balfour (in charge of provi-sions and stores). There is mail-truck communication with

Oodnadatta, three hundred miles away by desert track, every fourth week; and another route to the Finke River siding, two hundred miles north-east. Summer heat churns the long arid tracks into loose, difficult sand; and rare rains soften the sand and clay into slush and bog to hold up all movement for a week or more.

I had met the Reverend Mr Wright in Alice Springs, dressed in old clothes, well on in years, breaking down an army hut for removal over three hundred miles of road by truck.

Hospital cases of illness have to be transported by truck over the three hundred miles to Alice Springs, or by truck to either Kulgera or Erldunda Stations, and thence by the Flying Doctor plane operated and serviced by Eddie Connellan. The two-way radio transceiver gives at least a partial sense of security to far out Ernabella. It is the S O S and lifeline of the outback and, with the Flying Doctor Service, has saved many valuable lives and much suffering.

Choice of route from Ayers Rock back to civilization was difficult to decide. I had less than a fortnight to return to Brisbane, with many miles yet of slow camel travel before linking with faster transport. If I went to Ernabella, I might have but a day or so with them, with little hope of motor transport after the recent rains, and the probability of eighty or a hundred miles' walk against time to the nearest landing strip. If I went dead east, past Mount Conner, and on towards Erldunda Station, I would have some chance of a lift into Alice Springs by truck over the 'back' road from Oodnadatta to Alice Springs. Pastor Albrecht had advised me either to take the camels and continue with them to

Ernabella, or to ask Tiger to turn north-east to 'Andrews's country', vaguely forty-five miles over the sandhills from Ayers Rock.

But Tiger shook his head at mention of Andrews's country. He was keen to continue to Ernabella, probably to get in touch with old friends and display his importance; and Tamalji was also eager to return there where much of his boyhood had been spent. Thus I made my own decision. We would go straight in east to Mount Conner, and make a second choice at the first sign of regular traffic.

The slow journey from Ayers Rock to Conner was very much a repetition on a smaller scale of the country from Lake Amadeus to Ayers Rock, except that travelling natives had, for nearly half the sixty miles, burnt much of the thick spinifex a year or so before, laying bare the desert sand, over which was now sprouting a quick growth of flowering plants. There were hundreds of acres of the golden-green flowering grevillea, joy to Tamalji and Njunowa, who raced from corm to corm, sucking at the sticky syrup, and disturbing noisy grey martins. The desert was mostly clean, clear sand, light pink in colour, fitting background to the flowering daisies and heath along the sandhill crests. The lovely purple bloom of the parakeelia was spread out beneath the sun, and thus I had colour in the sand, and vivid colour in the plants, light high clouds and a blue sky, keen air, cool and fresh, and good company.

During the first day, Ayers Rock stood up huge and light mauve against the distant domes of blue Olga; and then Olga disappeared as we crossed a sandhill and we saw it no more. To eastward, Conner's flat top showed over wave after wave of low sandhills; and once again we played hide-and-seek. The distant tors were a never-ending source of inspiration and grandeur. It was difficult to understand how anyone could lose direction with such definite landmarks to follow; certainly not in winter's clear visibility. During the heat of summer, midday heat and mirage would distort landmarks and reduce visibility to a few miles. Half-way between them, both Ayers Rock and Mount Conner were clearly visible, and at no time during the three slow days were both the tors beyond sight from the crest of any sandhill.

After the half-way mark the spinifex was once again rank and unburned, and Tiger lit torches of spinifex to fire a string of jet-black smokes, which went racing away to northward, roaring, crackling, and leaping up in a wind from the south. The black columns of smoke rose well over a thousand feet; and during my wanderings from the camel line I crossed sandhill after sandhill to see answering smokes on every horizon other than in the west directly behind us. There was a grandeur and significance in this silent exchange of greetings and messages from one side of the desert to the other. There was no code, no prearranged order of signals, but each series of smokes told its own story. During the long hours of slow travel I decoded from a line of signals, rising one after the other down to the south-east, about fifty miles, that natives were on a walkabout, heading south to Ernabella, probably some of the big group still returning home leisurely from the Areyonga ceremonies. Forty miles or so to the south-west, a high, lone signal obviously indicated to Tiger that someone was hunting near the Pundijarrina Soak, north of the Musgraves. Directly northward, smoke swirled up during the day, clamouring for notice. It turned out later that they were on Andrews's country, known as Curtain Springs, the exact whereabouts of which was unknown to Tiger. Andrews's exact locality is known to very few. He is the 'farthest-out' settler at the end of a very rough, very sandy desert road. The most prominent signals were those rising in opposition to the northern smokes, from a spot which I concluded to be Weetabilla (Witabala) Rockhole, mapped about fifteen miles southwest of Mount Conner. The smokes conveyed a definite message to the three boys. They were obviously anxious to make personal contact with the signallers. There was much muttering, and some attempt to swing the camels. I watched Tamalji closely. He was endeavouring to persuade Tiger to head for Weetabilla, and then on to Ernabella. I intervened and ordered a direct course for Conner, which was now standing up squarely and unmistakably ahead. It was one mass of fractured rock, surrounded by high barren cliffs, supporting its own plateau high above the surrounding country. It was bright red above a thick forest of dark-green mulga at its western base.

Through the afternoon of the second day we headed for Conner. The boys fired a great amount of spinifex, until we had a continuous screen of smoke behind us, defining our straightened course to all distant watchers; and then towards evening the signals at Weetabilla commenced to creep out and extend one by one, up towards Mount Conner. The signaller was also now on the march. This strange converging of two lines of travel went on silently

209

over the desert; it was weird, crystal clear, and filled with meaning.

Tiger spoke seriously after evening meal and grace. I knew it was coming.

'Maybe white man got little cattle station close by Mount Conner. Aneri Soak – I think. S'pose we get there tomorrow. We get good water – might be fresh beef, too. Might be motor-truck there, take you to Alice Springs catch that aeroplane.' He turned in the dusk and indicated that Aneri Soak was a couple of miles south of Conner, and my map confirmed his point. The names on the map were few and far between; but Aneri Soak appeared beyond doubt. I was also curious to see who the signaller was.

We camped that night in a mulga thicket, where wandering natives had been digging holes three and four feet deep in the sandy clay beneath the mulgas, in search of the large bulbous honey-ant. The first cattle track I had seen for more than a week passed right beside the camp site, evidently made by a wandering bullock lured into the desert during the heavy rains, only to be cut off from reliable water-supply.

We got away at daylight and headed a little south of Conner. Tamalji and Njunowa immediately lit a string of smokes and got a quick answer from Aneri Soak. Our other mystery traveller from Weetabilla was obviously waiting there. The signallers to south, south-west, and to northward were not on duty or were disgusted; but faint smudges many miles off to the east on the cattle country about Erldunda answered us for an hour or two. Conner now towered high within three miles, when the camels quickened pace on to a rough motor track, the first I had seen for several weeks; and within a few seconds they were stepping out to the good pace of nearly three and a half miles an hour.

Although desert country still extended for many miles, the motor tracks indicated at least an isolated settlement. A large, heavy-tyred truck had passed about two days before, apparently going north-north-west. The track was seldom used. Within another mile we topped a rocky ridge, then passed over a curving sandhill that was one of a circle of dunes surrounding a saucer depression about three miles across. Just beyond the lowest point, a windmill whirled beside a trough and yards, and farther up the sandy rise a bare, square shed seemed naked and out of place. Beyond that again, several native wurlies dotted the sandhill.

'Who lives here, Tiger?'

'Dunno. White man, I think. Maybe white woman.'

I left the camels and walked quickly ahead. As often occurs near a rare watering-place, all plant-life had been eaten out except for an emerald-green wet patch sloping gently down like a vivid mat laid over the sand from the east. It carried the seepage from Aneri Soak on to a broad clay-pan in the bottom of the depression. The country was so much like a great saucer that the camels must have been seen immediately they topped the sandhill rim behind me; and I felt very obvious and wondered what manner of person or persons I might meet, as I walked a mile or so right out in the barren, sandy open, past the windmill, up past the yards, past a mulgabough meat-shed, and towards the hut, which was walled with flattened oil-drum sides,

211

thatched with mud over iron, windowless, with an open dark doorway; and not much larger than a household garage. The place seemed deserted, but I was conscious of being watched from the shadowy interior. A white woman, with a young child beside her, came into the doorway; and native women and children moved about the hut, while others peered round the corners of the building.

'Good morning,' I greeted her. 'I've just come in from Ayers Rock.'

'Well, you're just in time for dinner,' she said with amazing calm. 'Come right in!' Then she commenced to talk rapidly, made a pot of tea, and handed rations to several native women, who quickly scampered. The hut was stuffy, crammed with stove and tables, cases of provisions, a make-shift safe, curtained bed, shelves, and sewing-machine. It was evidently living-room, lounge, kitchen, store, office, and harness-room. 'You must have come a long way,' she continued. 'I wondered who was sending smokes up in the desert. You didn't have to turn back like the other party. Only went back from here a few days ago. Got this far in their four-wheel-drive trucks – bogged twenty-seven times between Erldunda and here. Used too much petrol and couldn't go on. We've had inches of rain – take tea? Got no milk, and sugar's short – Yes, they were going to try to drive to Ayers Rock. Schoolboys and some masters from Geelong College. Chap with a funny name – Becher-vaise – it was – keen on climbing hills. Anyway, they all went up Mount Conner and had a look at Ayers Rock from the distance – Have some corned beef? Haven't got much to offer you. Supplies are held up – don't hold back now.

ABOVE: The amazing formation of eroded terraces and bird caverns high up on the northern cliffs of Ayers Rock. This feature is about six hundred feet high, and is visible nearly fifty miles away on a clear day.

BELOW: The Old Woman's Cave, beneath the northern base of Ayers Rock. The cave undermines the cliff for nearly a quarter of a mile.

ABOVE: Approaching Ayers Rock from the north-east. The rock is about fifteen miles distant, glowing pink above the dark green of the mulga.

CENTRE: The south-western shoulder of Ayers Rock, with mulga plain beyond.

BELOW: An important native spring at the northern base of Ayers Rock.

It's good to see someone. Anyhow, some of the party talked of walking to Ayers Rock, but Mr Dumas – that's the man who helps here with my husband – they're away now on Erldunda, well-sinking for Mr Staines, and they're held up, too, with trucks bogged and broken down – anyhow, he warned them off the walking business. No surface water, and the desert's bad walking – have some pickles on your corned beef? That bread's just new and fresh. Must take some with you. Have some treacle. Sorry I haven't any jam. That's been off the tucker list for a few weeks.'

'Is there a direct track from here to Ernabella?' I asked. 'If I could arrange quick transport I should like to go there if at all possible, but I have only a few days left to get back to Alice Springs.'

'You'll have a job getting from here to Ernabella,' she informed me. 'Track's bad. It's nearly a hundred miles, and Ernabella truck is probably bogged down, too. My husband's camp is about thirty miles along the Erldunda road. You might get a lift in from there when it dries a bit more. The track you came in by goes up to Andrews's place – twenty-five miles from here, away back over the desert. He's got two trucks; but one's in at the Alice, and the other's broken down or bogged somewhere on the desert track somewhere this side of Henbury. He can't help you. My furniture's over at the Andrewses', and I've been hoping and looking for someone to bring it along. Not much chance yet awhile. Been down to Adelaide a couple of months ago, had a big operation; and just got back – got a match, I'll light me a cigarette!'

Somehow, the black tea and corned beef and dried

bread and pickles tasted like a banquet. The woman was more than middle-aged, and busied herself in the small hut as she talked.

'You haven't told me your name, or the name of your property here?' I asked.

'Name's de Conlay; and this is our Mount Conner Station – a thousand square miles. We've got some good cattle. Been here three years. Bit tough to start; but we're not sorry. A couple of years, and we'll be on the pig's back.'

Mrs de Conlay chattered on, breaking off now and then to talk to native women who padded in and out. Then she went and stood in the doorway, and watched my camels squatting near an isolated mulga a quarter of a mile away. 'Your boys all right? I'll give you some fresh beef for them. Got a killer in a couple of days ago. Had to. Natives on walkabout hopped in and pinched most of what I had the week before. Poor beggars. They go walkabout from station to station, and you feel you *must* give them some sort of a hand-out. Don't know that it does them any good, though.'

Mrs de Conlay asked me to stay the night; but time was too limited, and all hope of getting quick transport to Alice Springs was vanishing. She continued:

'I wondered why more natives came in this morning. Seem to know your boys. Quite a pow-wow going on. Trouble is, where tucker's concerned, they're likely to help themselves. There's another way you can go, if you don't reckon on going to Erldunda – by the mail track up to Angas Downs, fifty miles by old camel pad and sixty miles round the motor track – up there past Mount Conner.' She pointed to the north past Conner's great, flat-topped red mass.

214

'A lad from here rides it up and back every fortnight for the mail – leaves here Sunday morning, gets back Wednesday night if he's lucky. Connellan's mail-plane lands at Angas Downs next Tuesday week and you'd get a lift straight into the Alice. Plane was a week late last time. Lad had his ride for nothing. The plane set out and had to go back – landing grounds too boggy. I'll call a boy in to point out the proper way for you. What about staying the night and going on in the morning?'

Once again I declined her invitation. The urgency of contact with Alice Springs was paramount; but the next few minutes dragged on into an hour, unknown and unnoticed, as I persuaded Mrs de Conlay to tell me more of her story.

Paddy and Phyllis de Conlay took up the Mount Conner lease in October 1943, when they were both forty-five years old, and set out in an old camel-buggy from Mr H. J. Kitto's Mount Cavanagh Station. They travelled ninety miles a little west of north and reached Aneri Soak on Christmas Day 1943. No water was visible, so they dug frantically down several feet to a vile-smelling liquid. Paddy de Conlay dug on through the night, and early next morning, with his wife bumping up and down on top of endless petrol-drums placed to hold back seeping sand, bottomed on a bed of limestone and struck good water.

Then they celebrated their Christmas dinner one day late, of tinned foods and a bottle of beer given them as a blessing by Mrs Coulthard of Kulgera Station.

Building materials were out of the question; and during the heat of January and February the de Conlays decided to go underground, and in four weeks of hard work the two

215

of them had excavated a small room fifteen by ten feet, with an approach, in light limestone. They then carted mulga saplings in the camel-buggy, built a frame above the open cut and piled three feet of grass on to it, over which they packed a six-inch coating of clay from a nearby clay-pan. They then fitted the drive with a heavy bush-timber door, and dug a fireplace in one end of the so-called all-purpose room, Mrs de Conlay cooked under the open sky in camp-ovens. They locked up their few possessions, and went off in the camel-buggy for a better transport system, returning some months later with a borrowed donkey team and wagon loaded to the hilt with a windmill, pump, stove, and general supplies. Three weeks later they turned south-east to Kulgera Station, broke in a plant of stock horses given to them by Messrs Kitto and Coulthard, and then proceeded to Alice Springs to purchase a small herd of cattle.

In their absence wandering natives broke into their store and took £50 worth of supplies. It was a hard blow.

Mrs de Conlay dreams of the day when a proud home-stead will have Mount Conner as its background. Her present iron shed dwelling is hot and stuffy in summer, cold and exposed to desert winds in winter. The Andrews family are the nearest neighbours, twenty-five miles north-west by bush track. The nearest radio transceiver is at Erldunda, ninety miles away, and the nearest telephone two hundred miles away. No one lives to the west or south-west, for hundreds of miles, and the nearest township, Alice Springs, is 'about two hundred and fifty miles by road' – a road that begins as a desert track, continues as one through soft sand for more than a hundred miles before it jumps up on to rocky hill country, rough, slow to travel on, lonely, sometimes a week or fortnight passing without being travelled over.

One place in Australia still to be conquered.

The curving vertical sandstone strata of the north-eastern corner of Ayers Rock.

ABOVE: Some of the lower and more easterly domes of the Mount Olga group.

BELOW: An isolated northern dome of the Olga group, nearly a mile from the camera, with conglomerate boulders on the crest of a smaller dome in the foreground.

CHAPTER XXIII
NORTHWARD TO
BILL LIDDLE'S PLACE

The boys were not anxious to continue without a couple of days' 'spell'. Their desert friend from Weetabilla, and other natives, were busy bartering knives and oddments for some of Tamalji's pituri, and for a few minutes it looked as if Tiger's requests to Tamalji and Njunowa to 'go fetchem in camella', would provoke a blunt refusal; but they got up slowly with heavy scowls and grunts, and went towards the soak, while the strange natives stood muttering and making signs of extreme annoyance.

Within half an hour we were heading north, past the western overhang of Conner, silent and moody perhaps in the hot afternoon sun; and it was not until well towards evening that Tamalji gave a great, prolonged grunt of disgust, then a loud sigh of acceptance. It was as if he had cast off his moodiness like a cloak. He suddenly put his head back, commenced to laugh loud, and then louder, into his terrifying, bloodcurdling scream.

It was a great relief. From then on the three men were in laughing mood, chattering, and full of humour at the smallest incident. In reward we feasted that night on tinned fruit, seeded raisins, and routine meat, damper, syrup, potatoes, and onions. Their musical 'Xanku – good tuckout that one,' fully forgave me for driving them so hurriedly from Aneri Soak.

Ol' Man Camel was tiring and developing a bad limp. His original load had lessened considerably. It was not now necessary to carry more than ten gallons of water, and the tucker-boxes were dwindling day by day. Tamalji's bundles of pituri probably weighed a hundredweight. They were strewn all over the camels like a green market garden. Lady-in-Waiting was causing some concern again; but still there was no calf to greet the early-morning camel boy.

East and north of Conner there are salt-pans, clay-pans, and small salt lakes, surrounded by acres of salt-bush camel herbage. Most of the pans had already dried and caked into mud and brine.

The day after leaving Conner we moved along sandhill crests running north. The camels, four in line, padded in silent silhouette against a changing, troubled, wispy sky of cirrus clouds. At midday I pointed to dark smoke-signals northward of our route, crossing in from the west. The boys became excited again, pushed and coaxed the camels, and sent up answering signals; but the mystery travellers ahead were in a hurry, and passed about three miles ahead of us. We crossed their tracks – two horsemen, heading east.

Tiger turned the camels over a big sandhill, and up beside a lake about five miles long. Its shallow waters, gathered during the recent rains, were fast receding, gleaming in the sun. I walked cautiously over a perfect beach fifty yards wide, onto clean yellow sand, wet and hard, and out into the ruffled water, which might have been in any sheltered inlet on the coast of Australia. There I set a small stick, and watched the water recede fully twenty feet within half an hour. It was difficult to realize that it was the centre of Australia, and that within a week or so the sheet of water stretching away several miles ahead of me would evaporate down to a vivid-white salt residue, hot and barren, glaring, ugly, and treacherous. Myriads of minute creatures like pin-head tadpoles live in the clear, greenish water. The natives know them as 'Pupilja'. In a few more days they would be burnt by the heat of the midday sun, but no doubt leaving behind them some connecting link in the chain of life to emerge in their millions next time it rained and flooded the country.

To the north-west the low, long Basedow Ranges, named by W. H. Tietkins in 1890 after the anthropologist Herbert Basedow, M.A., M.D., Ph.D., B.Sc., etc., gradually rose from a dark-blue line on the horizon.

'We catch Wilbia Wells just off that point.' Tiger pointed to the eastern end of the Basedow. 'Road from Andrews's country must come in that way. We catch him properly. Long time ago this country belong to Bill Liddle and Snow Pearce – they have plenty sheepee, but pappy-dawg eat sheepee and native shepherd lose too many. All cattle country now; and some country – nothing.'

But there were many more sandhills and troughs, and mulga, mallee, and desert-oak thickets, with a few isolated clumps of gidyea; and some miles of rabbit warrens, dangerous to the camels. It was good witchetty-grub country, and Tamalji and Njunowa knocked low *Acacia Kempeana* (witchetty) bushes over, and pulled from the fractured roots white grubs as big as a man's finger. Their appetites were insatiable. They ate grubs and wild fruits during the day, and consumed all the meat, damper, and vegetables I gave them at night.

We crossed Andrews's bush track near Wilbia just after sunrise on the third morning from Conner. The main well was beside an old deserted bough-shed, and water was fifteen feet down in solid rock. It stank and was covered with scum. The place was depressing and indicated loss and failure.

'This water no good,' Tiger announced. 'Make you guts ache properly. Runabout all day. *No good!* Think we go quick for Bill Liddle's place. Catch him tonight – sun about there.' He pointed to four o'clock sun position in the western sky. 'Maybe have properly rest at Bill Liddle's. He got fresh meat, nanny-goata and bullocky. Maybe you get truck for Alice Springs. Aeroplane come next Tuesday. Mail-day then for everybody.'

I left the camels and moved ahead on a defined track, and within three miles met a string of well-bred horses, driven by several natives and a well-spoken half-caste who introduced himself as Arthur Liddle.

221

'Keep straight ahead,' he informed me. 'You'll find dad and my brother Milton well-sinking this side of the homestead. It's our eighteenth hole without striking water.'

The camel pad joined a sandy motor track that wound in and out of the sandhills. It was tough going, hot, monotonous, with the Basedow dropping behind and a few isolated hills rising northward; but even at its worst the desert country seldom remains without interest for long. On the crest of a very ordinary sandhill I rested before a very ordinary view, and heard a tiny bell-like note. A small crimson chat, blood red with light-brown wings, came within a few feet, dropped its wings and fussed. It obviously had a nest close by, and I spent nearly half an hour searching every bush and clump of spinifex without success while the bird kept within a few feet. Other small twitterers of the interior came round. Goodness only knows where they get water, or how they live through the heat of summer except by sucking at any morning dew. A brilliant golden bird of the same size flew past, followed by several others – the golden or orange chat.

The top of the sandhill for nearly a furlong was teeming with life. I walked slowly along it, accompanied for some distance by agitated feathered friends, until I found a small *Moloch horridus* about five inches long, with all his spikes and horns, lying doggo at the base of a small bush. Known as 'Entarkuma' by the natives, the Moloch lives out in the open barren rocks and sandhills, sleepy and tame, living on ants, coloured to the background he moves in. I picked up Mr or Mrs *Moloch horridus* and put it on my knee for several minutes while I sat and watched it feign sleepiness and unconcern; but every now and then it opened one small pin-head black eye, to take a cautious peep at its captor.

I placed Moloch at the base of a flowering bush and walked off, passing a deserted shepherd's camp two or three hours later; and continued, mile after mile, until I topped a rocky ridge. Within a hundred yards, Pioneer Bill Liddle and his half-caste son Milton were sinking a bore with a plant driven by motor-truck. They had chosen a place where, to the inexperienced, all sign of water was as far away as the moon.

We drove along a narrow valley between sharp ridges, through a gap, and up to Angas Downs homestead with its barn-like iron buildings and outsheds, windmill, troughs, stockyard and goat-pen; and small vegetable gardens cared for by half-caste women, and full-blooded natives and half-castes walking and standing about.

I sat with my hosts late into the night and pored over maps and photographs, and discussed the native question, particularly the problem of the half-caste. The Liddles, father and sons, are fierce barrackers for full recognition of half-castes as whites; but they could not see that although many white people are prepared to treat the unfortunate people of the third Australian race as 'brothers' in Christianity, they are not prepared to accept them as brothers-and sisters-in-law. It is one simple fact so often overlooked, which is an obstacle against a policy of breeding the black strain out of the half-caste on into the white race, rather than encouraging the white strain to fade slowly back into the black.

Liddle, sen. had wandered far and wide, and built homesteads, yards, and tracks for others who had failed, leaving him as the one remaining far-out pioneer of a large area. He was proud of his landing field, and of the fact that Connellan's planes landed there and left mail-bags for the Andrewses and the de Conlays. He is one of Central Australia's best-known bushmen, and knows the Centre far and wide. Old Bill Liddle, as he is generally known, is now standing by in the hope that his sons may be allowed to carry on as Australian citizens.

CHAPTER XXIV
DESERT WALK

There was little hope of any lift into Alice Springs, except by plane on the Tuesday. It was now Wednesday. Liddle had one truck away stranded, and the other being used as the power unit for well-sinking. He explained that Andrews had 'gone in' over the sandhills in a small truck to rescue a larger one that had broken down in the desert. There might be a truck in from Tempe Downs, sixty miles to the north, a good two days' hard journey by camel over the roughest, softest desert road in the Northern Territory.

Maps showed Henbury Station on the Finke River, sixty miles a little north of east by direct air-line across a terrible wilderness of sandhills without order, and occasional stone ridges. From Henbury it might be possible to intercept a vehicle on the rough southern road to Alice Springs.

'If you go by Tempe and Middleton Ponds, it's about ninety-five miles,' Liddle explained. 'If you go nearly back to Wilbia Wells, and then follow Andrews's desert track in – but that way's rough – it's about eighty-five miles.'

'And what if I go straight across country?'

'What – walk?'

I nodded, and explained that I did not want to take the camels any farther. One had a sore back, one was lame, and Lady-in-Waiting might prove a burden. The suggestion rather overwhelmed Liddle and his son. Eventually, Bill Liddle answered: 'Don't think you'd do it much under eighty miles; but come outside awhile. We'll have a look round.' We scrambled over a low ridge of vertical sandstone to a jagged rock about a hundred feet above the surrounding country. The ridge continued on beyond the gap close by, rose to about two hundred feet and ran off into the east. Northward of it there was a great sea of thick mulga forest, with the darker domed tops of desert oaks here and there, and patches of pink sandhill crest like the patches of foam on a choppy sea. It was a tumbled mass of sand, waterless, but supporting a tremendous amount of tree- and plant-life that would only add to the difficulty of locating landmarks.

Old Bill Liddle turned and cupped his hands. His enormous voice boomed up the hillside.

'Pakunja! Pakunja!'

Within a few minutes a young native came running, barefooted, over the rough stones.

'Pakunja!' Liddle thundered. 'One time you take cattle to Henbury Station, thataway. Remember?' Liddle pointed to the east.

ABOVE: Homeward-bound along the crest of a desert sandhill
north of Mount Conner.

BELOW: Mrs de Conlay and grandchild at Mount Conner homestead,
Central Australia.

ABOVE: Alf Butler, pioneer owner of Mount Quinn Station,
a property of one thousand square miles on the Palmer River,
standing outside his shanty of old iron, boughs, clay, and rocks.

BELOW: Tempe Downs homestead, Palmer River, Krichauff Range,
Tempe is one of the oldest cattle stations in Central Australia.

The native grunted and nodded.

'Good. Well, show me where Mount Ormerod is.'

Pakunja paused. He stood silently for fully a minute looking over the vast sea of deep green now tinged with colour from the setting sun. The ridge we were on flared in the red light and disappeared over the horizon like an ancient wall. About twenty miles to northward a line of deep-blue pyramids peeped above the sandhills; and about sixty miles to northward the red ramparts of the James Range stood up in a thin purpling line above the green. Pakunja was a little puzzled. Eventually he raised a hand high, and slowly brought it down on stiffly extended arm towards the north-east.

'Maybe that one Ormerod.'

A long way off a tiny blue point rose over the trees.

Liddle's voice thundered again.

'Maybe be damned! This man might go walkabout that way. You must be sure. Is that one Mount Ormerod?'

'I think that one Mount Ormerod all right,' Pakunja answered.

I left several parcels with Liddle to put on the Tuesday plane, and promised to send a note on the plane with an account of the journey. He explained that the timbered desert continued east and north to the Palmer River, and was bisected at an angle by 'Andrews's track' which went through the long wall somewhere between fifteen and twenty miles dead east, and then continued north-east over rough ground to Alf Butler's Mount Quinn homestead on the Palmer River. 'Three miles west of Ormerod. Keep your eye skinned for Ormerod, and you won't go wrong,' he advised. 'You won't mistake it. It's like a tiered pyramid facing the west, standing up close to the Palmer River. That map you've got shows it twenty miles south of the river. That's all bunk.'

I filled two water-bottles and a quart billycan, discarded all unnecessary items to reduce the total load of food, cameras, and water to about forty pounds' weight, then went out and camped beside Tiger and Tamalji and Njunowa, who were sleeping in the sand near the camel-boxes. It was difficult to sleep. The walk ahead would be a fair test for the physical fitness I had gained during the past few weeks. Memory of the amazing scenery, and the story and work of the missionaries, of the Chalmers and de Conlay pioneers, kept crowding in. Sometimes a long walk is the best aid to clear thought.

Thus, at the faintest sign of grey light down in the east, and with most of the stars still bright and clear, I rose. Tiger stirred immediately and sat up to waken the others. I packed quickly, took my sleeping-bag across, dropped it at Tiger's feet. It was a tribute to his faithful service; then, on the spur of the moment, I took off my old sandshoes, in which I had walked to Ayers Rock, and while I stepped into new shoes, passed the old ones over to Tamalji. He grunted; and to Njunowa I passed over a bundle of clothes. Those three natives, one a baptized Christian, one a savage myall, and the other a fat, giggling irresponsible youth, moved in close in that dark hour before the dawn and shook hands. Not many words were said. We were all perhaps a little sorry to part.

A few seconds later I was groping through mulga- and

228

mallee-bushes into the shadowy east, scarcely able to see, feeling with outstretched hands, until the softness of a well-used cattle pad set off in the right direction.

It was not until I was at least three or four miles out, and grey light had defined the red and brown of the low ridge running parallel a hundred yards southward, that I realized the new shoes might have been better with a trial 'run-in'; but for the next couple of hours it was battle enough to wriggle through a network of brittle dead undergrowth, and negotiate rocky gullies, stony ridges, and isolated sand-drifts through which any sort of good pace was impossible.

By about 9 a.m. Angas Downs homestead was at least twelve miles behind. A stony ridge lay ahead. I climbed it, sat beneath a low bush and took my shoes off. On the right foot a blister had risen two inches across, and another on the left foot an inch across – the first since boyhood. It was annoying, but so far the second skin had not been penetrated. With a razor-blade I slashed the backs and sides of the shoes. It gave some relief, but the damage was done; the rest of the journey would be somewhat of a hobble. Breakfast was all out of tins: a tin of peaches, a tin of condensed milk, and a tin of meat; iron rations with a vengeance.

There was no sign whatever of Mount Ormerod.

Down a little south of east a prominent range had risen into view. It was unmapped. Well to the north-north-west, the blue pyramid peaks still stood up on the skyline. By no stretch of the imagination could any one of them be Ormerod, whose direction was supposed to be north-east. I had no compass; but the sun's direction was definite.

Pakunja's tiny blue peak had disappeared somewhere in the mass of timber and sandhills.

A saltbush valley continued into the east, between ridges, in which I found four camels. I followed a faint camel pad a further two or three miles into sandhill country, softer, and with less order than any I had seen yet. It was as though mammoth lorries had tipped giant heaps of sand all over the world's surface, and planted all the scratchy spinifex and dead twigs of the world on them, leaving only the windswept tops of the higher sandhills bare and pink.

The cool breeze of the early morning dropped and left an uncomfortable warmth, bearable at first, but by late morning scorching with all the heat of hell. It slowed me down, and it was with some relief that I slithered down a sandhill to land in two deep wheel-ruts twisting away into the north-east. It was a definite landmark, and promised some relief from the laborious sandhills. At least, if anything happened, a lift *might* eventuate.

I was soon harshly enlightened. Very few trucks had passed that way, sufficient only to leave the two deep wheel-marks in the soft sand. The tracks were not wide enough for comfortable walking, which necessitated similar muscular action and balance to that of a tightrope walker. I tried to walk with one foot in and one out of a rut, then both out of the rut, followed by both in; until time proved that the best method was to walk between the ruts in goose-step fashion over the prickly spinifex clumps, until that became more monotonous and irritating than I ever thought possible; then, for a change, down into the ruts again; on and on, a few hundred yards at a time, winding in and out and round sandhills along the bush track of a pioneer, who had been forced to take his own powerful vehicle only where the country would let him travel. I doubt if there is any rougher motor track in Australia. Sometimes it almost doubled back on itself, twisted well away to east or west, but always returned to the one constant, general direction, like a tortured reptile recoiling to strike into the north-west.

But there is no better time to meditate seriously than during a long walk. Problems and all manner of questions present themselves automatically for silent mental discussion and judgment. The result is always clear. More than a thousand miles of tramping over Australia's wild heart had made it obvious that its few hundred natives now have a good chance of continued survival. That fact alone indicates many future problems, and a different aspect on the white man's right to enjoy the amazing winter scenery of Central Australia. Some day the wild gorges and valleys, mountain crests, monoliths and lakes, will become world-famous. It is merely a matter of time and circumstance; and the main question to be decided is, would the advent of the sightseer in large numbers spell the doom of the native?

Thus I had plenty to think about, and somewhere about 2 p.m. I gladly flopped beneath a shady mulga. My feet were aching from the cramped shoes and the heat of the sun, which was pounding down with all the force of midsummer. I built a fire, which neither by accident nor design could upset my quart pot of precious water, and lunched on a tin of luncheon beef, condensed milk, and dried apricots, washed down by the scalding hot tea. It seems an odd paradox that man should sweat with pounding heat, and apply heat to heat, to bring about a delightful coolness in a desert in one of its mocking moods.

The temperature was probably well over a hundred in the shade, and the morning breeze had died away. There was still no sign of Mount Ormerod. Instead, a mile or so beyond the lunch camp, the track wound through scattered mulga and down a sandy slope, then up a long rise for several miles, with one large sandhill slightly higher than the one preceding it, until the increase in elevation was perhaps a hundred feet in a mile. It was a long, slow, hot plod, necessitating frequent rests; and all landmarks were hidden by the sandy crests. The mulga had disappeared, and stately, dark-topped desert oaks dotted the spinifex and sand every thirty or forty yards.

Towards sundown I came to a heap of about three tons of cement dumped beside the track. Another mile or so farther on a second lot had been dumped and covered with a tarpaulin, and there were tell-tale skid-marks, stop-and-start depressions in the sand, indicating truck trouble; a deserted campfire and overnight camp, a discarded tyre, footmarks of men and women in the sand; more heavy vehicle tracks in from the north-east, a turning in and out of the spinifex, and off again, probably towing the broken vehicle in for repairs – nearly two hundred miles to Alice Springs. The dumps of cement all along the track indicated an overloaded truck setting out with faith in dry weather; but unable to pull over the terrible sandhills and the boggy valleys between, the dumping at first of a ton or two, then another dumping, until the truck itself broke down, and Andrews had been forced to leave his precious cement out in a wet desert land, where normally it never rained in spring. It told a story of tragic effort and disappointment, a home delayed, money lost, and of time and elements dealing another hard blow at a pioneer.

Out in that mass of piled sand, once again, where was Mount Ormerod? For that matter where was any known mountain or hill? One of my maps showed white space for many miles round. The other indicated Mount Ormerod close by; and Bill Liddle had said it was wrong.

The track continued up and up, and I walked barely a mile at a time between rests, until I came to an abandoned red jeep beside another pile of cement and several boxes, one of which was filled with green shrivelled limes.

If ever Mr Andrews reads this he will know that half a dozen limes were bashed open on stones and sucked in succession, and another half-dozen squeezed into my remaining water-bottle; then I went slowly on, uphill to a rocky knoll, and descended it slowly to sit awhile and look for landmarks.

There they were, now on every horizon, but unmapped. According to one map Mount Ormerod was about where I sat; but the rocky knoll was far too insignificant to fit in, and the track wound away north-east of it, whereas the mountain I was seeking was supposed to be three miles east of the track! No! A sandy waste still lay ahead, and yet it held a fearful grandeur. It was late afternoon and there was nothing else to do but to continue on, slowly now, but with the cool of night at least approaching.

Somewhere towards midnight, blisters and legs threw in the sponge and demanded rest; and I ate a belated tea

233

of tinned meat and condensed milk. It was the last of the food. I had half a bottle of water left. Mount Ormerod *must* be sighted before midday. Meanwhile a few hours' dozing would be in order. I had come to a definite conclusion that the wilderness areas of Central Australia belong firstly to the natives, and to the white man only on sufferance.

A large black desert oak had fallen across clean sand. It made a good fire, which cast a glow weirdly outward, so that the dark trunks of surrounding desert oaks standing straight and proud, seemed like surrounding warriors; but sleep was easy and deep.

CHAPTER XXV
JOURNEY'S END

Within three hours after sunrise I had wandered slowly down
a long, monotonous mallee slope towards a blue pyramid
mountain three miles to the east, rising gradually higher as
I approached – Mount Ormerod! Mount Ormerod! It was
easy to repeat the name. It was unmistakable in feature;
sudden, bold, with a greyness running through the red. For
the past twenty miles or more the only animal tracks had
been those of wandering camels and kangaroos; now horse
and cattle marks crossed the deep wheel tracks; scattered
tufts of grass had been eaten down to the sand; and then
on over a broad sandy saddle to sight the winding course of
the tree-lined Palmer River – another mile, a wisp of smoke,
and the iron-roofed, stone huts of Mount Quoin* Station.
Old Alf Butler walked out to meet me.

---

* Mutikutara.

'Here, mate, you look a bit tired. Come right in – sit down there – tea and tucker's right ready. I'm just having a sort of late breakfast. Where'd you come from? Here – take your shoes off, and rest those feet.' They were welcome words. Mug after mug of tea went down, scalding hot, fresh and strong. No better tea was ever brewed. I didn't ask the brand. Alf Butler kept up a supply of freshly cooked prime beef and large slices of home-made bread. A tired, exhausted stomach would have revolted at the bread and meat and hot tea; but weeks of open air and solid exercise had made me thoroughly fit.

Alf Butler lives a lonely life in his clean little shack beside the southern bank of the Palmer River, with the usual retinue of natives and their families. He wanted me to stay overnight, but sore feet or not I had to get moving towards any spot where a radio message could be sent explaining my delay. Henbury Station was a little more than twenty miles east-north-east, by clear, hard road over many hills.

'It's just as well you came the way you did,' Alf Butler told me later. 'You'd have missed out on a truck from Tempe Downs. O'Brien managed to get in past here a couple of days ago. Daughter getting married in at the Alice. Fact is, you'll be lucky to get a lift from anywhere before the mail-plane comes to Henbury. Nobody's travelling unless they have to until the ground dries more, and half the trucks are bogged or broken down. Old Bob Buck might run you in. He's at his place – Doctor's Stones – twenty miles beyond Henbury. What about a horse from here on? I'll send a boy with you to bring it back.'

But I preferred to walk.

Alf Butler cut more large slices of beef and bread, piled them into my pack; and I left his little home at midday and walked out past clay-pans and waterholes to the Palmer River crossing, a mile eastward.

Mount Ormerod now rose a couple of miles southeast, in tiered formation, shimmering in the heat, red rock, and green spinifex; but I soon lost interest in it and crossed the river to a broad sandy flat north of it. Green grass took a welcome breeze and rippled it along over hundreds of acres. The sandy desert country lay south across the river. To northward, rocky hills, conical hills, square hills, long flat hills, escarpments, silhouetted their shapes against a jagged skyline. Alf Butler had told me not to worry about water. 'You'll find it all along the road right to Henbury. It's all good holding country.' It was in deep gullies and wayside pools, some as yellowed clay-pans with water thick as soup shortly to evaporate in the early summer heat; others beneath leaning trees and deep enough to last several months; all in sharp contrast to the enormous deposits of sand south of the river, where the same amount of rain had fallen and hissed its way deep into the sand, to become salt and brackish somewhere down in the bowels of the earth.

Each turn of the road revealed new colour and lengthening shadows of hill and valley and ravine. Blisters had long ceased to hurt, but pace was necessarily slow, with welcome halts every mile or so to fit in with hilltop panoramas.

Towards sunset I was bearing down the eastern easy slope of a divide between the Palmer and Finke River systems, towards the sharp teeth of a line of hills that were red and revealing in the last rays of the setting sun behind me; deep purple and blue depth of shadows promised a cold night. Roger's Pass lay ahead in the hills. A line of trees curved in a long boomerang to the hills. In that delicate film of coloured light the pass could have been two or twenty miles distant, and the hills five hundred or five thousand feet high. The pass was named by the explorer Ernest Giles during his return with Carmichael and Robinson from the George Gill Range, on Tuesday, 12 November 1872, in honour of a Mr Murray Roger of the Darling River.

The red faded to deep purple, the blue to darkness; the dark grey of dusk drifted up the sky over the eastern horizon so that the sharp hilltops and the narrow road stretching straight and darkly ahead remained the only visible things.

The passing of that night, half-way through Roger's Pass, was a miserable affair of mosquitoes, aching feet, a relentless, whipping, cold wind, and drizzling clouds passing darkly overhead between the looming black east and west bluffs of the pass. It took some minutes to get going before morning daylight conquered the darkness, along a road now hard and pebbly, through gates and fences so seldom seen in the heart of Australia that I stopped awhile at the first fence to stare in some stupefaction at the long line of posts marching up a bare ridge like a lot of black sticks silhouetted against the dawn sky.

The road led onto the main Alice Springs to Oodnadatta bush and desert track, at a corner of the Henbury landing field. Nearly a fortnight had passed since the flood rains, but only two heavy trucks and one tractor had left marks on the road; and several days might pass before the next.

Henbury Station is invisible from a distance. Only its high radio mast juts above the dense green river gums, and the road swings from riverside sandhills, nearly a quarter of a mile westward, before crossing the Finke. Water was still racing in a wide rapid nearly three feet deep. The homestead is set between large sandhills on the north bank; one of the sandhills fifty yards to the west, surmounted by a large water-tank, another a hundred yards north-west, and the most impressive of them all a hundred yards to the east, with a broad valley of sand and spinifex and desert oaks running into the north. A few yards from the front gate, set up oddly behind harness- and buggy-sheds, blacksmith's shop and store, a signpost points to Adelaide, nine hundred miles south, half-way across a continent of sand and desert and wayside lakes.

Mrs Ted Cooper, wife of the young manager, set a delayed breakfast before me in a modern kitchen that was crowded with new cakes, biscuits, scones, jellies, and all sorts of things for a party. The Cooper kids and their cousins, the Hodge kids from Alice Springs, were on school holidays. They were not shy, but healthy, fair-headed, and lively as crickets. 'Hey, what about coming out on the big sandhill with us. We run over the top, then jump right out, and slide down – nearly a hunred feet. It's beaut! Y' coming?'

Later on, perhaps; meanwhile tired feet needed a spell, and urgent messages had to be sent.

239

Reginald Pitts, of Alice Springs Flying Doctor Service, was calling: 'PU Henbury. Have you any traffic? PU Henbury. Have you any traffic? Over to you.'

Within a few seconds my messages had gone out over the air. Mr Pitts would relay them to the Alice Springs post-office, and from there they would go quicker, as I had proved several times, than many similar distances elsewhere in Australia. Mr Pitts was talking again, asking for river-crossing information. Had any vehicle passed in through Henbury? Was the Finke fordable? Had there been any rain? Alice Springs had recorded a sharp morning shower of eighty points; and someone wished to set out on a long journey, and wanted the latest information.

From 7.45 a.m. until 6 p.m. Alice Springs maintains contact with all its transceiver stations, and Mr Reginald Pitts distributes and receives the news of the land, receives requests for medical and other advice, passes out hints and answers. It is a two-way wireless service that, if situated in Sydney, would cover New South Wales and much of Victoria; and speak and hear to and from every little town, responding to emergency signal at any time, with an added advantage that a listener may talk with the central station on a routine plan or carry on prearranged conversations, known as 'skeds', with one or more parties over hundreds of miles. The one flaw to a stranger, which doesn't seem to worry the local users much, is that anyone on the circuit may listen in to business and private telegrams and messages passing to and fro. My sharp ears and wondering senses were amused at a message loud on the Henbury receiver to someone a long way south, the text of which went: 'If you are anywhere in the land of the living, for goodness' sake write.'

Henbury is one of the oldest and largest cattle properties along the mighty old Finke. It is no outback pioneer's shed. It has beaten the test of time and drought and flood and heat; and the newer buildings are of stone and concrete and plastered interior, roofed with iron instead of clay and daub; while older buildings of neatly axed timber slabs and cement floors are still in good condition. The station has electric light, refrigeration, running water, enclosed vegetable gardens boughed over to check the burning summer sun, flower gardens and a rich green lawn. A windy day blows sand in fine stinging swirls to maim and kill plants, and a hot day scorches all to ground level. Every flower has its price.

There is a brass plate on the Henbury front gate, naming Finke pioneers. Henbury has a native community, many of them Christians in the charge of evangelist Galaliel, trained and instructed from Hermannsburg; a contented lot, well fed and well trained.

A young native woman had brought in her week-old infant, shyly, for 'all them white missus to look at him first time'. She rocked the child to sleep in its small 'pitchi' of carved wood, beneath a pepperina-tree.

I lay under the spreading river gums of the Finke, and drifted into retrospect. Millions of gallons of precious water glinted in the late sunlight, swirled and slid past on a long journey, only to vanish in sand and salt. The red heart of Australia had cast its spell. Thousands believe it to be

241

a dead, useless land; but it is not dead. It is hard, tough, treacherous, wild, magnificent, beautiful – yet ugly sometimes in mood; filled with the greatest traditions Australia has of the past in its native legends, and the remnant dream people emerging slowly from the past towards a new but difficult order.

Millions of years ago it was an elevated land. Now there is a vast coloured skeleton from which much of the earth and rock has withered and eroded away. Australia's bared heart still rots slowly and quietly, very slowly, through the thousands of years.

Drought may sicken it; flood may dampen it; but it will never die. Some of the rugged peaks are still nearly five thousand feet above sea level. Some of the canyons, many hundreds of feet deep, are still unknown, holding natural rock formations that some day may be world-famous. It is all a past ceremonial ground and legendary dream source of the oldest and most primitive race of people still on this earth. All the main rock features, animals, and birds, are embodied in native stories; those stories must not pass from memory. Pulverizing stones and lost native weapons are scattered over the ridges and sandhills, and in the abandoned camps of the desert that may never be occupied again – for this strange, ancient people, whose strength and virility lay in their fierce worship of their own past, collapsed at the coming of the white man. A long Christian crusade has helped to save a small band of survivors to face a future still uncertain and crowded with known and unknown difficulties.

Close protection of this strange land is more than

necessary. It will be criminal tragedy if exploitation is allowed in terms of dividends only; for some day the heritage of a vast unspoiled wilderness will write its own value.

Thus my questions had received their answers; but many of the answers indicate another story that has yet to happen, chapter by chapter. It will be a strange story; for, to be happy, it must have no end.

Text Classics

textclassics.com.au